# A GENIE RUINS EVERYTHING

Revised Edition, 2022.

ISBN: 978-0-9982120-7-4 (print)

ISBN: 978-0-9982120-6-7 (e-book)

Fonts: Plane Crash (licensed from WMKart.com), Garamond, Abadi MT Condensed Light, Curlz MT.

Visit the author's website at www.martina-fetzer.com.

Cover by okdoodle.net. Edited by Ellen Campbell.

If you purchased this book without a cover, you need to take a long, hard look at the choices that led you to this moment.

# A GENIE RUINS EVERYTHING

**\*\***

## MARTINA FETZER

# CONTENT NOTE

This series is meant to be funny. Many of the characters have traumatic backgrounds and gruesome events sometimes happen, but none of these are described very graphically. That being said, content warnings for each book in the series are available at the author's website: martina-fetzer.com.

# TABLE OF CONTENTS

(Hi, person who reads the Table of Contents)

*For the Rule of Three*

# RECAP

Edward Smith doesn't have a unique name, but he's got one hell of a biography. Smith is a clone of his former self. He'd hoped to resurrect in a robot body, but people who accidentally kill themselves and end up with their souls trapped in a cloud computing framework forfeit the right to be picky. He has the most tragic of tragic backstories, but he's coping.

Arturo Brooks is a cyborg through no fault of his own, and he'd rather you not mention it. Though the transformation saved him from death, it didn't solve his various anxieties. Brooks's greatest desire—to live a normal, monster massacre-free life—is impossible in a world with routine monster massacres. The closest he could get was marrying Smith and adopting two time-displaced teenagers...

Patience Cloyce was hanged for witchcraft in Salem, Massachusetts. An immortality-granting time machine fixed that, and she traveled from 1692 to the present, where *almost* no one wants her dead. It's an immense improvement. She's always on the lookout for another preoccupation to help make sense of her new home and to replace her lapsed fervor for God punishing the wicked.

Lemon Jones evacuated Luna during a perilous rift in time and space. The moon survived, but Lemon chose not to return there, preferring the simpler life and music of the 2010s. She fits in well with present-day hipsters, playing lead violin for an alt-rock band called Pop Tart & the Activation Energy and routinely scouring riverbanks for repurposable trash.

They live in Brooklyn.

# PROLOGUE

An etched wooden plaque above the desk read 'Home Is Where the Heart Is,' and it was true. Susie Darkstick was at home, her heart safely tucked inside her chest. A woman with a penchant for melodrama, she sometimes wished it weren't.

The pile of dime novels and penny dreadfuls on her desk grew higher as she set yet another book down. It, like the others, offered no insight.

Susie didn't know much about the paranormal or about opening a detective agency, but she knew one thing with certainty: her husband Dev hadn't died of a heart attack. By most accounts, a diet that included more choco-cakes than vegetables and an exercise routine that didn't exist had caught up to the forty-year-old patent attorney. One hot summer day, Dev went to his firm's restroom. Two hot summer days later, when his assistant got back from vacation, he was found on the toilet, slumped against a seashell-adorned wicker shelf with a bundle of two-ply still wrapped around his fingers. On the floor lay his phone, battery dead, unable to display the sixty-seven missed messages from his wife.

Though the autopsy had been conclusive, Susie didn't buy it. Her late husband had never complained of chest pains, but he had complained about a mysterious sound in the very rest-room where he died. The KASHUUU sound Dev described led Susie on a four-month journey to discover the undiscoverable. Her stupidly thorough and thoroughly stupid research pinned her husband's death on the supernatural, and Susie believed that whatever soul-sucking creature had fed on Dev's soul had also fed on hundreds of New Yorkers since. After all, how could over one hundred and thirty people die each day in a city of only nine million?

Susie traded her Pilates class for mixed martial arts,

navigated the excruciating forms necessary to get a New York State concealed carry permit, and used Dev's gargantuan life insurance payout to stock up on incense and amulets. Only one thing went unchanged: her library of pulp fiction, which formed the basis of her persona. Susie was leather-clad, richly eyeshadowed, and ready to take on the world.

She had help. A gold necklace with a small, lamp-shaped charm fell at her chest, and she rubbed it between her fingers. Her genie had too many rules—no killing, no resurrection, no erotic fantasies involving more than three participants, and nothing to do with spiders—but Susie had unlimited wishes and an illimitable will.

Two words set her plot in motion. "I wish—"

# 1 / THE CYBORG HANDBOOK

There may or may not have been a genie in Brooklyn, but there was a cyborg prone to existential funk. Arturo Brooks envied people who knew, from an early age, what they wanted to do with their lives. The child who played with fire trucks and grew up to be a firefighter. The child who went from playing doctor into chiropractic medicine. Another whose dreams of being a dancer were realized every night on stage at Hot Dollz.

Brooks had never been one of those people. He had, for eight years, worked as a field agent and then as CEO for the Reticent, a top-secret paranormal research firm. That may seem like a wild success story, but it wasn't. It was a hasty, disaster-based promotion that went downhill, fast. And in the two years since he was let go, Brooks had been involved in the following: bartending at Flaming Saddles, teaching paranormal self-defense at CCNY, dogsitting, working the phone for a suicide hotline, working the phone for a sex hotline, artisanal gin-making, and a brief stint as a superhero.*

None of those jobs stuck, but the thirty-something's dissatisfaction did. Therapy was minimally helpful. Meditation even more minimally so. Brooks was a cyborg, but he didn't know what that entailed. It wasn't like anyone had ever given him a manual, and he was tired of feeling like abilities were being sprung upon him on the spot by a malevolent author. Thankfully, rather than sit around complaining about it for a few *more* years, Brooks had commissioned friend and good-with-computers person Erin Burroughs to solve the cyborg problem once and for all.

He didn't expect her to be so fast. A distinct knock at the

---

* See: *The Bedazzlers.*

door—three taps in TAP-taTAP succession—meant Burroughs would barge through any second. True to form, she let herself in, her overstuffed satchel getting caught in the doorway for a moment.

As she jarred her bag free, Brooks made a frantic dive for the remote, changed the station from the daytime talk show *Donna!*, and stood up from the couch.* He hid his embarrassment with faux outrage. "Why don't you ever text first? Eddie and I could have been banging in here."

"Nothing I haven't seen." Burroughs reached into her bag and presented him with a stack of paper, neatly stapled with a plastic cover sheet. "Your manual's done."

"It's been *one day*," Brooks said.

She brushed that off. "I did a brief stint as a tech writer." Like Brooks, Burroughs had a last name beginning with B and ending with S. Also like him, she had failed at numerous careers since the Reticent's downfall. Unlike him, she had no issues with her lack of direction. She just knew that anything was better than the testosterone-filled world of IT.

Brooks leafed through the booklet, full of diagrams and snippets of code. "That sounds awful."

Burroughs shrugged. Now the band manager for Pop Tart & the Activation Energy, she had a career that was equally unrewarding. She looked up to see *Real Gutter Skanks of the Jersey Shore* and grimaced. "*That's* awful."

"Background noise," Brooks offered. He would never admit that he was a regular viewer and was invested in the conflict between boardwalk waitresses Tammy and Mandy, so he flopped back down to read the first page—well, the first page after the tastefully designed cover page and detailed Table of Contents. No one ever reads the Table of Contents.

---

* Of note, the exclamation point in *Donna!* is not a testament to the show being exciting, but an actual part of the host's legal name, Donna! Vandroogenbroeck.

## THE CYBORG HANDBOOK

Congratulations on your new cyborg! Cyborgs don't last forever, but with care, your cyborg should live at least as long as the average human being born the same year.

### WARNINGS:

*DO NOT drown your cyborg.

*DO NOT set your cyborg on fire.

*DO NOT expose immortal humans to your cyborg. Doing do will render them mortal, and the manufacturer holds no liability.

*Your cyborg may suffer from existential dread. If this happens, contact the manufacturer about replacement or return.

*Your cyborg contains materials known to the state of California to cause cancer.

"I hate you," Brooks said.

Burroughs shrugged.

Brooks flipped through the manual, again ignoring the Table of Contents. "Is there anything in here about—?"

"The eyes? Yeah." Burroughs squinted to think on it. "Uh... page sixty-three."

Brooks had accidentally turned his right eye—naturally a deep brown—the same vibrant green color as his husband's, and he couldn't figure out how to fix it. He ran a finger along the page and mumbled as he took in the instructions. "Ugh. Seriously?"

*Factory reset*, he thought, and the problem was solved.

"Hey, it worked." Burroughs plopped down next to him. "I also have a security patch whenever you're ready. No more evil Puritan programming for you."

"How do I know you're not going to put some evil in?"

Burroughs grinned. "Trust me. If I wanted to turn you evil, I'd just tell everyone where your USB port is."

Brooks offered not his USB port, but a rapid blink. "I'll

take the patch eventually, but Eddie and the girls are going to be home any minute, and I'd rather they not walk in on me with my port up in the air—"

The minute arrived.

Smith stomped in first and hung his leather coat next to the door. Lemon and Patience didn't stomp, but did proceed to hang their coats as well. Lemon's was made of multicolored, repurposed rain boots, and Patience's resembled a floor-length black gown. While the girls removed their boots, Smith tracked street sludge over toward the couch. He had that week's cleaning duty, as well as a tendency to screw himself over.

"What a goddamn hassle," Smith said. "Do you know how hard it is to get declared undead?"

Brooks stared into his eyes. "You're a zombie now?"

Lemon, mid-sprint to the kitchen, snickered. Patience didn't get it, and she seated herself on a nearby chair. The gutter skanks of the Jersey Shore had to go, and she switched the channel to *AMERICA: The History* (Episode 59: "How the West Was Overrun by Aliens"). Host Marco Petrakis possessed the same wild ginger hair and dubious historic knowledge she did, and Patience was a fan.

Smith gave a puzzled look. "Zombies? What are you talking about?"

"You mean un-declared dead," Brooks said. "Declared undead would mean they diagnosed you as a zombie or a vampire or something."

In fact, it was completely possible to receive a diagnosis for zombieism or vampirism. Now that the entire planet was familiar with the creatures' existences, a number of industries had been propped up around such conditions. There was paranormal insurance to protect against attack, Blood Drinkers Anonymous for rehabilitation, humane and organic organ farming for the conscientious undead, ultra-chilled apartment complexes to minimize rot, and innumerable others.

The world economy was experiencing a boom period.

"Whatever," Smith said. He gestured for Burroughs to move over. She rolled her eyes but complied, and Smith flopped next to Brooks.

"It's done, though?" Brooks asked.

Smith jutted his chest out and tugged at the shoulders of his button-down. "I am legally alive."

Brooks roped him into a short hug. "Thank God."

Patience nodded. "Mr. Zane's blessings shine on us all."

Patience used to be a Puritan, but gave it up in the twenty-first century. Mostly. She now worshipped a billionaire named Godwin Zane (a.k.a. God), whom everyone else in the house (and most people, society-wide) hated for various reasons, one of which was his choice of a nickname. The group chose to ignore Patience when her cultish tendencies arose.

"You look normal again," Smith said, waving a finger at Brooks's eyes.

"About time, right?" Brooks asked.

"I don't know. What if I liked you better when you looked like me?"

"I can dye my hair blond," Brooks said dryly.

Smith faked a shudder. "As much as I love late-nineties teen heartthrobs, *and you know I do*, don't ever do that."

On screen, Marco Petrakis flailed his arms. "I think—I think—it's pretty clear. It's definitely clear. That when the authors of the American West described 'African Americans' they were really writing about aliens—"

Lemon returned from the kitchen, Pop-Tarts in hand, and seized the remote. "Nope. I can deal with the Zane thing and the country music, but not my ancestors being aliens."

Smith squinted. "I mean... *you're* from the moon, so..."

Brooks shut them both up at once. "Lemon, no food in the living room. Eddie—"

Lemon un-seized the remote and retreated, shaking her

head at the TV, where Marco was using play-by-play technology to draw a UFO on the painting *Gunfight at O.K. Corral*. Patience leaned in toward the screen, engrossed.

"What?" Smith asked.

"Seriously, come here," Brooks said. This time the hug lingered.

"*Come on*," Smith groaned. He loathed PDAs, and he eyed Burroughs eying them.

"Oh, don't mind me," Burroughs said.

"Why are you even here?" Smith asked. Before she could answer, he speculated. "You miss me so much you're trying to get some secondhand love from Brooksy? It's sad, really..."

She smacked his shoulder. "I finished that manual for your husband. *You're welcome.*"

Smith curled his lip and gave Brooks a guilty look. "About that—"

"What?" Brooks asked.

"We're gonna need to pop off to the courthouse for a quickie," Smith said.

"Why?"

"Well, it turns out weddings performed in the cloud with one dead groom aren't entirely legal."

"We're not married?" Brooks asked.

Smith shook his head. "Nope."

Lemon shouted from the next room. "Can I play your bachelor parties?"

"No," Brooks and Smith said at once.

Patience's strange sense of morality kicked in, and she frowned. "You're living in sin once more?"

"Never stopped," Smith laughed.

Burroughs changed the subject. "You guys are good to set up shop, though?"

Brooks nodded. "Now that Eddie's not dead, we can get a business license. You sure you don't want in on this?"

"Yeah. I'm sure," Burroughs said. For some, working for the Reticent had been a calling. For her, it had been a job— a job that plenty of people were doing these days. She felt no guilt in leaving it behind, and it would take a lot more than Brooks and Smith could pay to pull her back into investigating creatures that wanted her dead. After all, the detectives weren't loaded like Lemon, who played violin for Pop Tart & the Activation Energy, and whose brother routinely wired her thousands of dollars from the future.*

Patience shook her head and sighed quietly, which was as good as interrupting for her. She didn't typically offer unsolicited opinions, so Brooks took that as an opportunity to ask her opinion.

"What's wrong?" he asked.

"Hmm. Well. It strikes me as foolish to seek out demons and the like, given the circumstances."

Brooks didn't follow. "What circum—"

A loud PAKOW drowned out the end of his question.

Lemon dove under the kitchen table in her best infantry commander impression. "Duck! Duck! Duck!"

Everyone gawked at the kitchen. Unlike her, they recognized the sound as that of a passing car's backfiring exhaust.

"Goose?" Smith asked.

Brooks rolled his eyes. "Are you okay in there?"

Lemon crawled out from under the table and dusted herself off. "Yeah, I'm *grape jelly.*"

"You've been acting skittish lately," Brooks said.

"Yeah," Lemon said, joining them. "I have fans now."

Smith didn't follow. "So?"

"Well, everyone *else* in this house has died," Lemon said.

"Ah," Brooks said.

Patience folded her hands. "Those are the circumstances

---

* In 2202, 1000USD holds the same value as 20USD in 2016. Lemon's brother Tangelo was actually being cheap.

to which I referred."

Lemon glanced around, still nervous from the backfire. "What if someone tries to Billy Joe Swanson me?"

No one knew that Billy Joe Swanson had murdered the lead singer of Trebuchet, M.D. in 2031. The room shared a bewildered series of blinks.

Lemon tried another. "Tyler Xanzibar Booker?"

No one knew that Tyler Xanzibar Booker had murdered the lead singer of Musk Brats in 2024. Lemon may as well have been Marco Petrakis ranting about crop circles.

"Mark David Chapman?" Lemon wondered.

"Oh," Brooks said. "Okay."

"Yeah. That makes sense," Smith said.

Patience nodded. "The alien who abducted John Lennon."

Burroughs squinted. "I don't think he wa—"

"Let it go," Brooks said. He turned to Lemon. "Anyway. You're immortal unless I'm around, so how much do you really have to worry about?"

Lemon stared at Burroughs. "I'm home *a lot.*"

"I'm getting you more gigs," Burroughs said. "Hang in there."

"In the meantime, you're not going to die," Brooks said.

"She *could* die," Smith said.

Brooks stood. "Not helping."

"I'm just being realistic," Smith said.

"You're being an asshole." Brooks stepped toward the kitchen and put an arm around Lemon. "Listen. If anything dicey happens, I'm going to sprint as far from you girls as I can."

"You sure?" Lemon asked.

Brooks nodded. "I'm sure. Nobody's going to die."

# 2 / SOMEBODY DIES

The Little Achievers Academy smelled like peas. Not just in the lunchroom, where mushy peas were served five days a week, but in the hallways, the classrooms, the restrooms, and in the theater where Patience's Senior English poetry recital was taking place.

On stage, multicolored paper pom poms hung at varied lengths in front of a white-intentioned curtain that had yellowed from decades of exposure to cigarette smoke. No one was allowed to smoke in there now, of course, but there was no regulation about replacing draperies. Twenty-some people had gathered to watch the class performance, and they were scattered around a three hundred seat auditorium, trying their best to avoid both human interaction and scattered piles of smushed peas.

Toward the back of the room stood a sad construction paper sign taped to a cigarette butt receptacle:

> There's plenty of room!
> Please seat yourself toward
> the front of the theater.

Next to it, a mortal Lemon sat tucked between Brooks and Smith. This, she reasoned, would put them near the emergency exit and allow her adoptive fathers to act as bodyguards. As an undersized Goth kid droned on onstage, the three engaged in an informal contest to see who could roll their eyes the hardest.

"My pain," the Goth said. "I asked for barbeque. I got honey mustard. My pain."

"You know what would make this better?" Smith asked.

Brooks offered a dark answer. "Death?"

Smith, an alcoholic, offered his own. "Bourbon."

"Hoo boy," Lemon said.

"There's only three more, at most," Brooks said, stilling himself. As there was no program, their plan was to leave as soon as Patience was done. They kept hoping she wouldn't be last. "I think we'll make it."

"I might kill myself again," Smith said.

Brooks leaned over Lemon and snapped, "That's not funny."

"What, you can joke about dying but I can't?" Smith asked.

"Shh," Lemon said.

Brooks didn't shush. "*I* never killed myself, so yeah. Exactly."

"That's not fair," Smith said.

"Shhhhh," Lemon said again.

"I asked for Pepsi," the Goth said. "I got RC. My pain. My pain. My pain."

Two claps from the front of the auditorium were their cue to join in. Lemon offered up three whole claps, Brooks gave three half-claps, and Smith made a single, bitchy clap.

Ms. Flexor returned to the stage to present her next student. "Up next..." She hiccuped.

Smith snorted. "Even the teacher has to drink to get through this."

"...Up next is Miss Patience Cloyce."

"*Finally*," Brooks said.

Brooks and Smith clapped politely as Lemon wooed.

Patience was slow to reach the center of the stage. Her russet frock dragged and got caught on a few crooked pieces of plyboard, and her cheeks reddened as she paused to tug it free. When she finally made it, she cleared her throat and spoke meekly into the microphone.

"There was a tree upon whose branch I sat
Whilst fretting o'er the drowning of my friend
A friend whose crimes the witch trial did begat
And pondered would I also meet my end?
The briskness of the wind, a thing to please
But wind was not the source of my next chill
Men there from the future, traveled with ease
The situation had me feel quite ill
And go I must, the notice came to pass
To venture forth with nothing but myself
One final glance back toward the Salem grass
My life now fitting for any bookshelf
And so I think with every passing day
How blessed to meet the forest men so gay."

Brooks, Smith, and Lemon applauded, though none was particularly moved.

"Did she write a *sonnet?*" Brooks asked, confused.

Smith shrugged and said nothing as he tried to remember a single fact about sonnets.

Patience shuffled offstage, and Ms. Flexor returned to the microphone, wobbling under more inebriation than before. "Kids, right? What can you do?" The rest of the audience joined her in a chuckle. "Up next is Miss... Miss... Treximett Paddington, with some *nonfiction.*"

Outside the auditorium, in a lavender hallway with flickering fluorescent lights and finger painted "GO SPARTANS" banners, a still-blushing Patience met up with her family.

"That was taxing," she said.

"You did great," Brooks said.

Smith and Lemon nodded.

"You *toasted* it," Lemon said.

"I was again reprimanded for telling the truth," Patience said. "Ms. Flexor gave me a D."

"She's just mad she's not getting the D herself," Smith

said.

At points of extreme frustration—such as being subjected to a groanworthy pun—Brooks spoke Spanish. He muttered under his breath, "*Por qué es esta mi vida...*"

Patience didn't follow. "Regardless, I'm failing."

"Ehh, who cares?" Smith asked.

Brooks glowered at him. "*Who cares?*"

"She can form a sentence and use a calculator. That's about all school's good for," said Smith.

Brooks disagreed. "Just because *you* didn't learn anythi—"

"I learned all sorts of things." Smith winked.

Brooks groaned. "How she does in high school determines what she can do for college."

Smith snorted. "You think *Patience* is going to *college?*"

"Why wouldn't—"

Lemon was disinterested, and she buried herself in her tweets. Someone named Dijon had gone through her timeline and liked everything she'd ever tweeted—including a regrettable drunk tweet directed at House Speaker Paul Ryan—and she had to scour Dijon's timeline to assess the threat level.

Patience too was disinterested in talk of her future, and she shuffled across the hall to observe the newest addition to the school's trophy case: 3$^{rd}$ Place Regional Bumper Bowling. The plastic trophy featured a teen girl bowling with a smiley face emoji in place of a ball. Patience squinted to admire the obvious line where two sides of a mold had come together when a warm sensation hit the back of her neck. She let out a slight peep, not loud enough to alarm her family. Patience turned and found herself face-to-face with The Weird Kid.

Every school has one student who never seems to hang out with anyone and who is way too into some creepy hobby like collecting butterfly wings. With her burdensome frocks and prim sentences, Patience had been the Little Achievers Academy's Weird Kid until Kayden Desai showed up. His long, wavy black hair made more contact with his conversation partners than his black eyes did. True to form, Patience turned to look at him and he looked away.

"I believe your poem," he said, still gazing down the hallway. His voice was the tonal opposite of her high-pitched near squeaks.

"Hmm?" Patience wondered.

Kayden droned on. "I looked it up. Patience Cloyce lived in Salem, Massachusetts during the witch trials. The records say she was hanged but there's no record of a burial. I think you're her."

"I am indeed myself," Patience said.

Kayden brushed at his sleeve. "That's cool. Are you, like, immortal, or did you time travel?"

"Both," Patience chirped.

"That's cool." He brushed at his other sleeve. "You wanna go to Homecoming with me?"

Patience frowned. "I mustn't dance." It was one Puritan rule she still vehemently stuck to.

"That's cool. I was just gonna stand in the corner and watch people anyway," said Kayden.

"Oh," Patience said. "I can do that."

"I'll stop by your house then."

"Hmm. Do you have the address?" Patience asked.

"Yeah."

She didn't absorb that as creepy, and Kayden walked away. He pulled a handful of peas from his pocket and smeared them onto the wall as he left. Patience turned from the bumper bowling trophy and returned to her fathers' argument.

"Not everyone has to go to college," Smith said. He himself had nothing more than a GED, and he'd saved the entire world on no fewer than eight occasions.*

---

* He still didn't know what a sonnet was, though.

Brooks and Smith had been reading up on conflict management, and according to most notable psychiatrists and a few websites ending in .org, it was important to use 'I' statements and avoid accusation.

"*I feel like* you're being defensive because you didn't go to college," Brooks said.

"*I feel like* you think you're better than me because you did," Smith said.

"*I feel like* that's you projecting. I didn't even finish school."

"*I feel like* these 'I feel like' statements aren't working and I'm even more annoyed than I would have been without them," Smith said.

Brooks tilted his head. "I feel like you're right."

CRAAAASH.

The noise came from the auditorium. Brooks, Smith, and the girls rushed back inside to find twenty-some people taking cell phone pics of the stage, where a three hundred pound lighting fixture had fallen onto Ms. Flexor, crushing her. The audience could do nothing but watch as the puddle of blood beneath her spread. Her arm twitched for a moment, then was still. The Goth kid stepped back out onto the stage, absorbed what it was like to experience actual trauma, and turned around.

"*Brannon Braga*," Lemon exclaimed, looking above her head for more fixtures. "I'm out of here." With that, she flung the door open and took off down the hallway.

Patience put a hand in front of her mouth and spoke through it. "This is most terrible."

"It is," Brooks said. "But on the bright side, your whole class is probably getting As now."

# 3 / THE MOST DANGEROUS GAME

Ancient sepulchers and burial mounds seem like they'd be the places to find a genie. At least, Rhett and Solange Conner thought so. The newlyweds had been traveling for six months nonstop, seeking the last genie known to exist. Sumerian ruins held nothing. Irish passage tombs held nothing. Incan citadels held a pair of wrathful machukuna, but since the Conners were looking for a genie, those were as good as nothing.

Now they were in Manhattan. It was impossible to walk three blocks in New York without spotting a child practicing its new glitter induction superpowers or running into a half-orc seeking signatures for a petition. The paranormal was everywhere. But, like the catacombs and pyramids before it, the city was a bust on the genie front. For a pair of ex-Reticent employees, it was frustrating.

The Conners sat on a bench outside the Javits Center at dawn. The only creatures they had found there were vampires, which they had staked—vampire rights activists be damned.

Solange brushed some light grey dust from her dark brown skin. "Maybe next time."

Solange always tried to look on the bright side, and her husband loathed that. Before she could say more, Rhett began ranting. "How can it not be here? We've looked into every paradigm shift in the last year and not one is the djinn?"[*]

Solange considered that out loud. "Maybe it doesn't exist anymore."

---

[*] Djinn means the exact same thing as genie, but makes the person saying it feel intelligent and cultured.

"It. Exists. *You told me* it exists!"

"I told you it exist*ed*. I never said any still exist." She began to point out an inopportune fact. "We've never seen it, and we haven't met anyone who's seen it, so—"

He grabbed her by the shoulders and shook. "The djinn exists!" In spite of the rose-colored glasses with which his new wife saw him, Rhett was kind of a dick. He was especially so with a goatee full of vampire dust. It was the only hair he had, and that annoyed him even more. He let go of Solange and scratched at the underside of his nose. "The djinn exists—"

A few paces away, a pedestrian tossed a forty-eight ounce plastic cup onto the sidewalk.

Rhett leaped from the bench in a tizzy. "Hey!"

The pedestrian ignored him and kept walking.

"You see this?" Rhett asked. "*You see this?*"

Solange hopped up. "Mmhmm."

"We're gonna get that genie," Rhett said. "And when we do—" he pointed at the cup, "—things like that aren't going to happen anymore." A truck drove by, and its exhaust made him cough. "Things like that, either!"

Solange walked over to the cup, picked it up, and tossed it in a nearby garbage can. She returned to Rhett's side.

"There's one lead left to chase," she said, raising a hopeful finger. "A couple of detectives who keep getting way too many lucky breaks?"

Rhett knew very well what their last resort was, but he wanted nothing to do with it. He groused, "You think I don't know? *I know.*"

"So we're heading to Brooklyn," Solange said.

Rhett scowled. "Brooklyn."

# 4 / ADHOC

Faking someone's death is a classic insurance scam. But as it became increasingly common in a world full of immortal and immoral creatures, so too did methods of spotting it. Brooks never had Smith declared dead (on account of the fact that he was secretly still alive in the cloud), but Lemon had. She thought she was doing her distraught father a favor by handling paperwork that Brooks was too upset to tackle. To make a short story shorter, Brooks was not allowed to keep the life insurance payout, and actually had to pay back extra due to "fraudulent activity." They could have asked Lemon for help, since she was flush with cash and this was entirely her fault, but Brooks felt a parent asking their child for money was "gauche." So he and Smith were about to open their business at a financial low point.

The Piedmont Building was perfect for that. A multi-use facility constructed in 1957, its rent was as cheap as its asbestos was abundant. Three floors—below, at, and above ground level—contained two dozen offices, each with a frosted glass door. All of the building's accents, from doorknobs to lighting fixtures to the shared micro-shower, were faux gold and chipping. It looked like the interior of Trump Tower, if it had been run through a post-apocalyptic wasteland.* Occupants included three unlicensed massage therapists, half a dozen attorneys, a singing telegram service, a tarot card reader, and a playing card reader.

One office on the lowest level† now had two names pasted across its frosted glass:

---

* That wouldn't happen until 2052.
† Read: Basement.

## ADHOC AGENCY
## EDWARD SMITH
## ARTURO BROOKS

Inside, the office was cramped and windowless. Brooks and Smith sat at opposite ends of a wood veneer desk, the former typing away at a laptop and the latter sifting through piles of hardcopy paperwork, which was somehow still a thing in 2016. Aside from the desk and chairs, the only furniture was a large, sad bookcase with shelves buckled under the weight of absolutely nothing. It stood on Smith's end of the room, leaving a narrow gap between it and the desk that Smith constantly struggled to fit through. There wasn't much wall, but a pile of paint swatches rested on the desk anyway because Brooks was resolved to cover up Corporate Beige.

Brooks was a poor typist, and Smith couldn't bear another minute of his two-fingered technique.

"What's the point of being a cyborg if you have to use a computer?" Smith asked.

Brooks looked up for the sole purpose of rolling his eyes. He wanted as little to do with being a cyborg as possible, and Smith knew it. With the knowledge in his new manual, Brooks had turned off every cyborg feature he could without shutting himself down. No GPS, no internet access, no randomly changing eye colors. Just Arturo Brooks, the way he was supposed to be, but with a USB port.

A few more poorly paced taps at the keyboard, and Brooks said with enthusiasm, "That's it. Everything's filed."

Brooks and Smith were officially, with all the paperwork it entailed, proud founders of the Agency for Detecting Horrible Occult Crimes, or ADHOC. Smith had insisted there be an acronym because "all the best things have acronyms." His examples had been BBQ and BJ.*

Smith set down one of many brochures they picked up at the small business office. On its face, a happy white woman held a happy white baby under the text "Healthcare and You!"

"Did you realize we have to have health insurance?" Smith asked.

Brooks didn't look up from his laptop to respond. "Yeah."

"That's stupid," Smith grumbled.

Brooks, now busy registering a business email address, shrugged him off. "Everyone needs it."

"You're a cyborg, the girls are immortal, and I'm suicidal. We don't need health insurance," Smith said.

Brooks looked up and blinked. "I think that last thing means you do." He closed his laptop and slid it toward the center of the desk. "You're kidding, right?"

"I'm fine," Smith said. "You can't handle dark humor anymore?"

"Again... *Seriously*... It's not funny after you actually kill yourself."

"*Accidentally*," Smith said.

"*Eddie*."

"I got better." Killing himself hadn't been what it was cracked up to be, and Smith spoke with as much sincerity as he could muster. "I'm fine."

"You'd better be. I'm trying this thing where I talk to you about stuff before it spirals out of control and somebody jumps off a bridge or gets magmatized or..."

"And by 'somebody' you mean me," Smith said.

Brooks verbally tip-toed. "I'm not saying I've never done anything stupid, but... yeah. I mean you."

"Well, what's the point of asking if you're not gonna

---

* When presented with counterexamples KKK and NAMBLA, he went quiet.

believe me?" Smith asked.

"Okay," Brooks said. "I believe you."*

"So the health insurance—"

"I looked through it earlier," Brooks said. "It says we get a huge discount if we get physicals and mentals."

Smith squinted. "Mentals?"

"Yeah, if—"

"I'm gonna stop you there because I know you're not suggesting I go to yet another shrink."

"I didn't *suggest* anything," Brooks said. "We're just talking."

"Good." Smith had gone to therapy exactly twice. The second time, he had accidentally killed himself trying to prove that he was immortal. The first time, the therapist tried to pry the bi away on behalf of his overly religious adoptive parents. They eventually changed their homophobic minds, but he no longer spoke to them, mainly because they thought he was dead. And so, while Smith was willing to give "I feel like" statements a try, he refused to ever set foot in a therapist's office again.

Brooks grabbed the healthcare packet and started suggesting. "It's not all shrinks."

"Brooksy—" Smith warned.

"It's not. They accept 'alternative mental medicine.'"

Smith's jaw slacked. "What the hell is that?"

"We can go someplace with healing crystals and epsom salt baths and it counts. So long as the primary purpose is—" he picked up and read from the brochure, "'—to enhance the mental or spiritual well-being of the patient.'"

"You want me to go to a woo-woo doctor?"

"We can go together and make fun of the whole thing," said Brooks.

Smith pondered that. "I do like making fun of people's

---

* He didn't.

earnest beliefs."

Brooks pumped his fist. "That's the spirit."

"How big's the discount?" Smith asked.

Brooks enunciated slowly, for emphasis. "Twenty percent."

"That's... a lot of discount."

"Yeah. So what do you say?"

"I say we won't be on the same plan if we don't pop over to the courthouse," Smith said. "Are you trying to Spider-Man me or what?"

"What does that even mean?" Brooks asked, certain he didn't want to know.

In dying, Smith had made great strides in moving beyond the brand of toxic masculinity that drove him to drink too much and listen to thrash metal. Unfortunately, he resurrected into smug, matter-of-fact nerdiness. "I never told you about that? Like ten years ago, some editor decided that married Spider-Man was boring, so they had him sell his marriage to the devil, basically, and then he and MJ would never remember they were married, and—"

Brooks was very, very bored.

Smith picked up on that and got to the point. "You're not trying to renege, are you?"

"You could have just worded it that way from the beginning. And no," Brooks said. "I've just been too busy with all *this* paperwork to think about even more paperwork."

Smith had no concept of how much paperwork Brooks had done, and he dismissed the idea. "Uh huh."

Brooks dismissed the dismissal. "Oh, for—"

"I'm just saying—"

Brooks interrupted. "I know what you're sayin—"

Smith re-interrupted. "*I'm just saying,* getting married was *so* important to you, and now—"

"You think it's not important to me now?" It was important. So important that Brooks activated his HUD to pull up his calendar. Of course, Smith couldn't see that.

*Business, Business... Patience's Birthday.*

"Thursday," Brooks said. "You, me, and a courthouse."

Smith was not a timely person, and he forgot a lot of plans. But for this he pulled out his phone and navigated its cracked surface to set a reminder. "Okay. Thursday." His voice was more confident than he was. Thursday left six days for things to go horribly wrong.

# 5 / BAND ON THE RUIN

On Saturday, Pop Tart & the Activation Energy had their first sellout show. Flopsy's capacity was sixty-five (standing room only), and it was packed with early twenty-somethings holding craft beer and blowing marshmallow biscotti vapor into the air. Brooks, Smith, and Patience were the last ticketholders to arrive inside the narrow building, and they gathered in the back. Patience balanced on her tiptoes, trying to catch a glimpse of anything at all, but it was hopeless.

"You're sure this is how you want to spend your birthday?" Brooks asked.

"I'm unused to celebrating birthdays," Patience said. The closest she'd come in her Puritan days was a baptismal retrospection. "I'd rather the evening's attention be drawn to Lemon than to myself."

"You at least want us to push our way to the front so you can see?" Brooks asked.

Patience blushed. "With your permission, I wish to stand with friends."

"When did you get friends?" Smith asked.

Brooks nudged him, but kept his eyes on Patience. "You're an adult now. You can hang out with whoever you want."

"Thank you, sirs." Patience began what would become a long journey to the front of the crowd. She tapped a woman's shoulder, muttered, "Excuse me, but I must convene with my friends," and, when she was let through, tapped the next shoulder in her path. "Excuse me, but I must convene—"

"When *did* she get friends?" Brooks asked.

"How weird do you think they are?" Smith asked in turn.

"Super weird..." Brooks trailed off.

In the crowd, he spotted a mid-twenties hipster wrangling two small children into staying close to him for the show.

There were many more interesting things happening, but Brooks's attention stayed on this lumberjack-bearded dad.

"I don't get why more people don't use those kid leashes," Smith said.

Brooks groaned but remained transfixed.

"Hey." Smith waved a hand in front of Brooks's face to stop the pining. "No."

"No, what?" Brooks asked.

"No babies. No small kids. No."

"I didn't say anything," Brooks said. "For all you know, I was admiring Paul Bunyan."

"Not your type," Smith said.

"And my type is...?"

Smith used both hands to point to himself. "Chubby old dudes."

"Okay. You caught me."

"I know I did," Smith said. "You're on this kick again?"

"It's not a *kick*. The girls are adults, and two years of parenting isn't exactly what I had in mind."

"That was the compromise. We've been over this a hundred times," Smith said. "Maybe more."

"Yeah. 'It's not fair to force some kid into knowing about monsters.' Well, thanks to you the whole world knows."

Smith recalled his part in revealing vampires to the world and somehow turned paler. "I wasn't thinking..."

"It doesn't matter," Brooks said. "Everyone would have found out anyway since giant holes keep opening up over Manhattan and people are tagging orcs on Instagram. But now that everyone knows weird stuff exists, we're normal."

"I wouldn't go that far," Smith said, certain it was still weird to have two time traveling immortals, a cyborg, and a clone living under one roof.

Brooks shook his head. "What I mean is, we don't have to worry about our paranormal stuff screwing some poor kid up. Every kid is going to be screwed up. There's no more debate over 'do you tell them so they're prepared to fight or let them have a normal childhood?' It's all solved."

"If you think it was just the paranormal stuff, you have another *think* coming."

Brooks ignored the pun and put on a mocking tone. "*Oh, I had a bad childhood.* Lots of people did, Eddie."

"A bad childhood is being poor and getting slapped around," Smith said. "I'd think you, of all people, might understand better than that."

If Trauma were an Olympic event, the world would be a sick place. Also, Smith would have a gold medal. Brooks, only having witnessed his family get torn apart by wraiths, would lose in the match for bronze. He couldn't fathom Smith's issues or why he refused to talk about them, so he sighed in frustration. "How would I understand when you never talk to me about *anything* that bothers you?"

"I do so. I told you all about the line at the DMV and that shitty Spider-Man story," Smith said.

"*You know what I mean.* You're still burying things instead of trying to work through them."

Smith shot him a warning glance, but before he could say anything, Pop Tart & the Activation Energy took the stage to the shrieking of two intentionally mistuned violins. The band didn't have a backdrop or lighting effects, but they made up for it with frantic movement on the stage. All of them but Lemon, anyway. Her violining was listless compared to Jaxx Onomy's, and it looked even more pathetic next to the dramatic flourishes of drummer Miranda Huffenstump. In addition, she kept doing a weird thing where she looked up for falling lighting fixtures.

The crowd didn't notice as they nodded along to the clanging and screeching instruments.

Trevor Tarte grabbed the mic and put moderate vocal talent to Lemon's words: "*I missss the futurrrrrrreeee... Don't like the passssst...*"

"That's not subtle," Smith said.

Brooks shook his head. "We should talk to her."

After suffering through the entire setlist and three unrequested encores of the same song ("Life of an Olympic Curling Champion"), Brooks and Smith made their way down a cinderblock hallway with low ceilings, ducking to avoid hitting their heads on light bulbs hanging precariously from lone wires. The backstage area wasn't what either man expected. Through a chipped wooden doorway with no door, they found Pop Tart & the Activation Energy.

SNORRRT. Trevor Tarte did a line of coke off the stomach of a very naked Miranda Huffenstump, who giggled and pawed at him in return. Lin Ho slumped over a table in the corner, passed out next to a half-eaten bowl of Fruity Crunch Nuggets cereal he'd topped with Baileys instead of milk. Jaxx Onomy was nowhere to be seen, as he was busy vomiting in the bathroom.

Brooks stood in the doorway, appalled. "What the hell?"

Lemon looked up from her chair, where she was reading more tweets. "Oh, hey."

Smith scoffed. "*Oh hey*? You never said your band was a VH1 *Behind the Music* waiting to happen."

"The fame's getting to them," Lemon said.

"The fame...?" Smith trailed off. "Whatever. We noticed your lyrics."

"And?" Lemon asked.

SNORRRRRRRT. Miranda giggled again.

"Maybe not here," Brooks said, motioning behind himself.

Lemon dragged herself off her chair and followed them back into the hallway. In an adjacent bathroom, Jaxx Onomy let out a wall-piercing RETTTTTTTCH.

"Are you okay?" Brooks asked.

Lemon leaned against the wall. "The past *sucks*. Transit is slow and cops are racist and I can't even go to the Hornstag Retreat in the Vega system."

"So you wanna go back to the future?" Smith asked.

"No," Lemon sighed. "Didn't you hear us play 'I Don't Miss the Future'? The moon *sucks too*. The food's all kale and everyone has to serve in the Lunan Army."

Brooks patted her shoulder. "I know what's wrong."

"What?" Lemon asked.

"The honeymoon period is over. At first, it was all trees and hipster fun, and now you're in the day-to-day grind."

"The honeymoon period?" Lemon asked.

"Oh yeah," Smith said. "You're doing the same thing day in and day out."

Brooks nodded. "Play a show, send a tweet. Play a show, send a tweet."

That was an accurate portrayal of Lemon's life, and she nodded.

Smith patted her other shoulder. "You have to find the next thing to be excited about."

"I don't think *you're* one to take advice from," Lemon said.

Smith responded with a short grunt. That a nineteen-year-old could identify him as a bad influence didn't bother him, but it should have.

"Well, definitely don't try to kill the ennui with booze and suicide," Brooks said. "But he's right. If Pop Tart & the Activation Energy isn't doing it for you anymore, you have to find something that will."

Smith stepped toward Lemon, bumped into a light bulb, and stepped back. "Let me ask you something."

Lemon nodded.

"You grew up listening to Pop Tart & the Activation Energy. You were their biggest fan. What happened to the Lemon who was in the band?"

Brooks shook his head. "We're not doing spoilers—"

"Just one," Smith said. He turned back to Lemon. "I'm sure you watched some special or read a biography or something. What happened to Lemon?"

"No one knows," Lemon said. "After the election of—"

"Spoilers," Brooks said.

"No one knows," Lemon repeated. She left it at that.

Smith nodded. "Then it seems like you have some wiggle room to do your next big thing."

"Take ADHOC for example—" Brooks didn't get to finish.

"You're right." Lemon had an idea what her big thing might be. "I think—"

Lemon didn't get to finish either. A CLAAAAAANK, CRSSSSSH, and handful of screams interrupted from the direction of the club.

"What *now?*" Smith asked.

The three of them scurried toward the noise, Lemon keeping behind her fathers. Burroughs stopped them at the stage entrance. "Stay back there. Keep the band back there."

"Why?" Lemon asked.

"A lighting fixture just fell on one of the crew," Burroughs said. "Craziest thing. The police and ambulance are on their way."

Lemon glanced up, searching for additional fixtures.

"Is he dead?" Brooks asked.

"Oh, he's definitely dead," Burroughs said.

"What are the odds of that happening twice in one week?" Smith asked. When there was no reply, he stared at Brooks. "What are the odds?"

Brooks pursed his lips and inhaled loudly before answering. "Do you *seriously* want me to calculate the odds for you?"

"No." Smith shrugged. "I don't like it, though."

"Me neither," Brooks said.

He silently activated his calculator and found the odds to be quite low.

# 6 / NO MONEY MO PROBLEMS

Though their office was tiny, Brooks felt compelled to use some of its space for décor. If he didn't, he knew Smith would try to achieve his vision of creating a crazy wall with newspaper clippings and yarn. It was Monday—ADHOC's first official day of business—and Brooks dumped the contents of a small tote bag across the desk: an artificial aloe, a few knickknacks, a framed business license, and a framed photo of the two detectives taken back when fedoras were merely frowned upon rather than completely unacceptable. Smith stopped stocking the bookshelf and eyed a third, empty picture frame.

"What's the empty one for?" he asked.

"For framing our first dollar," Brooks said.

"You think people are gonna pay cash?" Smith asked, handling the frame.

"It's a *symbolic* dollar. Once we have a paying client, I'll just put whatever dollar in there."

Smith blinked. "But why?"

"It's *symbolic*."

"Of what?" Smith asked.

Brooks wasn't sure. "You know. Business?"

Smith set the frame back down. "I changed my mind. I don't want to remarry you."

Brooks glowered.

There was an almost inaudible knock at the door and the knob rattled. Their security system had been designed by an idiot, so Brooks tapped the button on their desk that unlocked the door. As it opened, a buzzer sounded with a BLORRRRN.

Brooks shut his eyes and pressed his lips together, trying to remain calm. "I thought you were going to change the chime?"

Smith shrugged as he settled in his seat. "It's attention-grabbing."

Their first client seemed to agree, as he had ducked back out into the hallway.

Brooks swept the decorations out of the way and took his own seat. He adjusted his tie. "Come in. It's fine."

There was another BLORRRRN as the man re-opened the door. He was a wiry, nervous type, and he fiddled with his hands after he took a seat across from the detectives.

"What can we help you with?" Brooks asked. His voice was pleasant and he beamed with the thought of having their first client.

The man chewed at his lip. "You're detectives Brooks and Smith?"

Smith resisted the urge to ask whether the man had "read the fucking door."

Brooks extended a hand that went unshaken.

"Arturo Brooks," he said.

Smith nodded. "The other one. And you are?"

"Clayborn Finley," the man said. "I hear you help with... weird cases."

"Yeah, that's what we do," Smith said.

Clayborn's eyes darted around the room. "Are there any microwaves in here?"

"What?" Brooks wondered. "No."

Clayborn seemed relieved, even as he nervously tapped his fingers on the desk. "Good, good. We can talk here."

Smith started to say something. "Why wouldn't—"

Brooks nudged him quiet. If there was one thing he knew from working mindless service jobs, it was that the customer was always an idiot but it was best to tolerate it.

"I have a problem," Clayborn said, still tapping.

"Whatever it is, it's not too weird for us," Brooks said, still bringing the cheer.

"You have no idea how glad I am you said that," Clayborn said. Then he announced his problem, "Globalist zombies are poisoning our brains."

Brooks blinked a few times. "What?"

"Have you seen a zombie?" Smith asked.

"Well... no." Clayborn stopped tapping and brought a hand to his mouth to chew at a fingernail.

"How do you know they're poisoning you?" Smith asked.

"Chemtrails," Clayborn said between nibbles.

"Oh no," Brooks said. His face became that of a seasoned traveler realizing the only nearby restaurant was a McCormick and Schmick's.

"Oh no?" Clayborn pulled his hand away from his mouth, frowned, and clenched his fists. "They've gotten to you. You're shills." He leaned toward the desk, concerned. "Have you been drinking tap water?"

"What?" Brooks asked.

"Tell me you haven't been drinking tap water. It'll poison you and make you gay."

Brooks pretended to clutch an invisible pearl necklace. "Oh my God. Is *that* why I like sucking dick?"

Smith shrugged a shoulder. "He does."

Clayborn stumbled backward out of his chair and pointed at the detectives. "Shills! Shills! It's too late!"

"Yeah, we can't help you," Smith said. He pointed his thumb at Brooks. "This one's even voting for Shillary."

Clayborn backed toward the doorway, his eyes fixed on the globalist cucks before him. A BLORRRRN spooked him out of the office and he scurried away.

When he was gone, Brooks turned to Smith. "You're not going to vote for her?"

"I've never voted for anything in my life, and I'm sure as hell not gonna start now," said Smith.

"This one's important."

Smith rolled his eyes. "You say that every four years."

"It's true every four years," Brooks said. In fact, there are much more important local elections every year, but like most Americans, he only paid attention when there was a presidency on the line.

A knock at the door, a button press, another BLORRRRN.

They looked up to find a new customer in the doorway. This one was a short, angry woman. The former trait was evident just looking at her; the latter became evident when she stomped into the room, threw her handbag down, and huffed as she took a seat across from the detectives.

Brooks began the introduction. "Hi. Arturo Br—"

"I know who you are," she said. "My husband's been abducted by ghosts."

The men shared a confused glance. Ghosts, being noncorporeal, could not abduct anyone. They mostly hung around cemeteries, sobbing over their own graves.

"What makes you think it was a ghost?" Smith asked.

"He disappeared," she said, handing over a silver Zanephone. "Look at this."

"It's a phone," Brooks said.

"Denny's phone," she said. "Look at his search history."

They did, and it looked like this:

Ghosting
Ghost
How to Ghost Someone

Brooks spoke through gritted teeth. "I see."

"Yeah, we can't help with this," Smith said.

The woman squinted. "Why not?"

"Check the search results. Denny left you," Smith said.

"No, he didn't," the woman said.

Brooks handed the phone back to her. "Yeah, he did."

She got up to leave, scoffing, "This is ridiculous. Some paranormal detectives." On her way out, she slammed the door shut and shouted back at them, "I'm going to see Susie Darkstick!"

"Who?" Brooks asked.

"Beats me," Smith said. "You have a lock screen on your phone, right?"

Brooks nodded. "I do. Don't you?"

"Obviously," Smith said. "Maybe we should find Denny and teach him how to use a fucking cell phone."

Brooks raised his brows. "You want to help someone get away with doing their spouse dirty?"

"Not if you put it that way," Smith said quietly.

"Well, the good news is we're busy for our first day," Brooks said.

Smith jumped at the opportunity to finish that thought. "The bad news is we're busy with a bunch of lunatics."

"Right," Brooks said. He glanced at Smith, who was fiddling with his tablet. Out of nowhere, it began playing a trite pop-punk number.

*When there's nothing you can dooooo*
*And the world is turned against youuuuu*
*You wish for someone you could calllll*
*To kill the pain of it allllll*

"What are you doing?" Brooks asked. He knew Smith's taste in music was bad, but he didn't think it was *that* bad.

"I didn't do it," Smith said. "I looked up Susie Darkstick's website. It's autoplaying this shit." He held the screen up. "Look."

*Breeeeeaaaaathe it in*
*The sadness in your liiiiiife*
*Breaaaaaaaaathe it in*
*Pain that cuts like a kniiiiiiife*

If the site had an aesthetic, it was that of a teen vampire drama. Pink and black abounded, and the fonts were almost illegible in their quest to look Gothic. What the detectives could make out read: "Susie Darkstick, Esq. When darkness sticks it to you, darkstick it back."

Brooks grimaced, scooched toward Smith's tablet, and closed the tab. The emo singer was cut off at a word that was either pain or drain. Either would have fit the refrain.

Smith set the tablet down and smirked. "We have competition. Are you worried?"

"I'm quaking," Brooks said dryly.

Smith put a hand on his shoulder. "Need me to calm you down?"

"How long have we been open?" asked Brooks.

"Uh... forty-five minutes," Smith said.

"You're incredible."

"That's a good adverb," Smith said. "I'll take it."

"It's an adjective, and I'm not sleeping with you during business hours," said Brooks.

"Fine." Smith's eyes shifted. "What's an adverb?"

"It doesn't matter," Brooks said snippily.

BLORRRRN announced the arrival of two more would-be customers: a pair of blonde college roommates, as fit as they were frightened.

Smith found them, unlike the last two patrons, worthy of greeting. "Heeeyyy—"

Brooks glared at him and stole the conversation. "Arturo Brooks. That's Edward Smith. He's a pervert. What can we do for you?"

"Our apartment is haunted," one said.

The other nodded. "Super haunted."

"What makes you think that?" Brooks asked.

"Our beds, like, move themselves and sometimes there's a creepy face in the mirror."

This was promising, and the men shared a knowing glance.

"That sounds like a haunting," Smith said. "Probably a ghoul—"

"Yeah, we know," one said. "That's kind of why we're here."

"The base fee is two hundred," Brooks said. "It's fifty an hour if the investigation goes beyon—"

The first blonde's face scrunched. "We have to pay?"

Smith squinted at her. "This isn't a charity—"

The second blonde cut in. "Susie Darkstick doesn't charge."

"Okay?" Brooks said. "We do."

"Remember the Six Block Disaster?" Smith asked, bringing up one of the eight times he'd saved the world.

"Yeah, like sixteen thousand people died," the second blonde said.

"It would have been billions if it weren't for us," Smith said. "We stopped that. Not Susie Fuckstick."

"Darkstick," the first blonde corrected.

She turned to leave and her roommate did likewise.

"We're going to go see Susie," she said.

"Fine. We don't care," Brooks said. In just under an hour, every speck of cheer he had to offer had disappeared, replaced with irritability.

When the co-eds were gone, Smith turned to Brooks. "We do care, right?"

"Oh, absolutely. We *have* to go see what this Darkstick business is about."

# 7 / LIFE GOALS

Patience's bedroom was unlike Susie Darkstick's website. Before she'd moved in with Brooks and Smith, the room had been a nine-by-ten-foot dusty storage space with an inclined ceiling and one tiny window. They cleared out most of the dust, but Patience had resisted any attempts to decorate the space and had actually requested that the carpeting be removed. They wouldn't let her have a dirt floor, so she chose rustic wood. When it came time to paint the room, she chose Tasteful Gray. When it came time to add curtains, she shunned them all, stating that she was "meant to rise with the sun." Her twin bed—its mattress the stiffest allowed by law—was adorned only with a set of brown sheets and a horsehair-stuffed pillow. Her legs dangled off the edge of that bed while she looked at her phone.

TAPTAP. Her cracked bedroom door flew open before Patience could say "come in."

She tossed her phone toward the horsehair pillow and grabbed a nearby science textbook (*Remedial Biology for Seniors Who Just Need to Graduate Already*). Her hands were their usual color, but Patience was caught red-faced. She was supposed to be studying, and she was ashamed.

Lemon stood in the doorway, looking down at her. "What are you doing?"

Patience turned to chapter six (*Humans Don't Have Gills*).

"Studying," she said. Patience didn't lie. But it wasn't a lie, she reasoned, if the book was open.

"Yuh huh," Lemon said. She eyed the phone at the head of the bed, its alert light blinking. "What were you *really* doing?"

Patience lowered her head. "Texting."

"Why would you need to hide that?" Lemon asked. Then

she realized, and her eyes bulged. "You were texting a *guy*."

Patience flushed harder as Lemon hopped a little victory hop.

Lemon engaged in rampant speculation. "Who is he? Is he in your grade? Is he a she? A they? I shouldn't assume. Is it the Goth with the soda poem? The weird one with the peas?"

Patience fanned herself with the textbook. "I don't wish to discuss it."

"I do," Lemon said. She grabbed the textbook from her sister's hands, tossed it aside, and sat down next to her. "I gotta vet this creep."

"Why did you come into my room?" Patience asked.

Lemon was thoroughly distracted. "Something about us starting our own detective thing. It's *flab trash*. I'm over it. Let's move on to the guy thing. Have you been on a date yet?"

"We are not formally courting," Patience said. "We did rendezvous at your show on Saturday, though."

"*Ooooh*," Lemon said. "This is perfect. I was thinking about being a life coach..."

When she was certain there was no more to Lemon's sentence, Patience spoke. "I thought you wished to be in a band, or become a detective." She pondered. "Or perhaps go to school for veterinary medicine. Or open a fortune-telling booth. Or drive an Uber. Or—"

Lemon acknowledged her abundant, fleeting whims. "Yeah, but I also thought of this just now."

Patience lacked the boldness to glare, but her lip curled almost imperceptibly.

"It's perfect," Lemon said. "You don't know what to do with school or relationships or anything, and I'm really bored. I'm gonna be your life coach."

"What does a life coach do?" Patience asked.

There's an old adage: those who can... live; those who can't... coach lives. What Lemon could have said was that the job of a life coach is to live vicariously through those they're coaching. Instead, she offered, "Coach you. On life."

Patience shrank as she thought about the time Lemon dragged her on a vampire-staking adventure. They couldn't die, so they didn't nearly get killed, but it was an uncomfortable time for all involved. "What does that entail?" she asked.

"First off, I've gotta meet this guy," Lemon said. She hopped up off the bed.

"But—"

"I've gotta. Come on." Lemon grabbed Patience's arm and forced her to stand.

Patience planted her feet, which would have been easier had she left the carpeting, and did her best to resist being dragged out of the room. But Lemon had nearly a foot of height and well over sixty pounds on her, even in the dress. It was hopeless.

# 8 / JINX ON THE LIRR

Brooks and Smith were also hopeless. It's indisputable that no New York City transit is less enjoyable than the Staten Island Ferry, but coming in at a close second is the LIRR. On Fridays, the trains are jam-packed with douchey, drunk yuppies heading for the Hamptons. On weekends, they're packed with obnoxious Long Islanders bounding into the city, yearning for entertainment. Whatever the day, the trains are slow and painful. An hour into a two-hour ride, Brooks and Smith had grown bored with sitting through screeching stop after screeching stop. Their boredom had reached the point that Smith, having beaten the last level of Hokeyblock Blast, was reading the news on his phone. Times were truly desperate.

If Brooks had a dollar for every time someone had coughed during their ride, he would have had twenty-three dollars. If he had twenty-three dollars, it still wouldn't be enough to pay for a better method of transportation to Stony Brook, New York. They were heading for the middle of no-where, population thirteen thousand.

"Oh my God," Brooks said.

His partner said that a lot, and nearly always with the same level of exasperation, so Smith didn't look up from his phone. "What?"

"I just realized we have to do this in reverse to get home. This is hell. I'm in hell." He swatted a fly that had landed on his pleather seat.

Smith stuffed the phone back into his pocket. "You still have access to The Afterlife™, don't you? Go hang out at Disneyworld or something."

Astute readers may recall that Smith died at one point. The Afterlife™ was a cloud-based afterlife system, now banned in most countries. It was where Smith lived, in Brooks's head, until they could get his new clone body sorted out. Brooks did still have access to its seventy-two virtual scenarios (including Disneyworld), but he was unamused.

"I'm not turning that back on," he said. "I'm finally normal again."

Setting aside some occasional HUD use, that was true.

"If you say so. But I can think of *another* way to pass the time," Smith said with a wink.

"We're *on a train*," Brooks said.

"A train with a bathroom," Smith said.

Brooks eyed the flickering light and peeling band stickers above them (Sugar Ray was the highlight of the bunch). "If this is the passenger compartment, I don't even want to know what the bathroom looks like."

"Live a little," Smith said.

"Oh, I'm living a *lot*. For instance, my shoe just discovered something. Is it a melted Big Gulp? Is it pee? Who knows?"*

"You're getting high-strung. Come on."

Brooks's eye twitched at the sound of *yet another* cough. A different passenger decided to deal with the noise by cranking up his headphones to the point that everyone in the train car could hear Trev Cracklin's twangy voice droning on about trucks and guns.

Brooks tugged Smith's sleeve and moved into the aisle. "Okay. Fine. Let's go."

They headed to the bathroom together, without discretion. No one cared.

Brooks entered first, muttering a pep talk. "Don't look at the toilet. Don't look at the toilet."

Smith followed him in. "See? It's not that bad."

Brooks glanced around what was essentially a glorified

---

* It was both, plus some melted snow dredged from boot treads the previous winter.

airplane bathroom. "The mirror is etched with a swastika."

"It was probably an edgy teenager, not an actual Nazi, if that helps," said Smith.

"It doesn't."

Brooks eyed a locked glass case on the wall. Under its cracked surface was a pristine, bright pink advertisement with some Gothic rose clipart. In Curlz MT font, it read:

Demon trouble?
Call SUSIE DARKSTICK.
877-GETSTICK.

"You've got to be kidding me," Brooks said.

"It's fine. No one's gonna see that ad. No one ever uses the toilet on this thing."

"How would you know—"

Smith put a hand to his chest as he reminisced. "I've done *so many* lines of coke on these cars."

"Classy." Brooks groaned. "Maybe you can join Pop Tart & the Activation Energy."

"Come on. You know I have no talents."

"Neither do they," Brooks said.

Smith snorted.

"That was rude. I didn't mean that."

"Yeah you did. They're terrible." Smith stated it like a fact, which it was.

"Still."

"Don't worry. I won't tell," Smith said.

Still feeling snippy from the everything, Brooks muttered under his breath, "You never do."

Smith heard that, and there was a brief silence as he worked his way up to conversation. He had a storied history of saving sincere talks for the worst possible locations. In one stunning example, he'd proposed to Brooks in an

Afterlife™ simulation of a Hitler Youth camp. This time was no different. He diverted his attention from a dramatic 'DO NOT DRINK THE WATER' sign to look into Brooks's eyes.

"You know I love you, right?"

Brooks blinked a few times. "I thought we came in here because you're horny."

"Well, yeah. But, I mean it..." Smith dodged eye contact. "If you need to be with someone else to get what you want out of life, you should do that."

Brooks grabbed Smith's chin and forced him to look at him. "What the hell are you talking about?"

"If you don't want to remarry me, I get it. I'm always gonna be the guy who's done coke on the LI-double-R. And there's shit you want to talk about that I can't. I *get* that."

"You really don't," Brooks said. "These things only come up because I know I'm going to be with you forever. It wouldn't be worth arguing otherwise."

"Okay..."

"We're going to the courthouse tomorrow," Brooks added.

"Okay..."

"You don't believe me," Brooks said. "Still."

"I *know* you. That honeymoon period spiel you gave Lemon was about you," Smith said.

Brooks rolled his entire head. "Oh, it was not—"

"You probably have a pro/con list somewhere," Smith said.

"I don't have a... physical... list."

"Uh huh."

Brooks put his hands on Smith's shoulders. "I don't know why you're convinced I want to get rid of you when we *just* opened a business together, but I don't. I promise."

Smith reached up and brushed the hands away. "Things are too good, Brooksy."

"*Oh my God.*"

Symptoms of PTSD differ, but Smith's most prominent was a persistent belief that nothing would ever be okay. His chest tightened as he spoke. "I'm serious. Not that someone has to die again like Lemon thinks, but we're sort of happy, and historically that doesn't bode well—"

"That wasn't at you." Brooks pointed at the toilet he'd been trying to avoid. "*Oh my God.*"

Smith took a step back, bumping into the sink. "Oh, fuck."

Peeking up from the toilet bowl was a bloated, decapitated head. The pair leaned over to inspect it. Male, South Asian, fifty-something.

"Dead," Brooks said. It may seem obvious, but in their line of work they couldn't assume.

"No blood," Smith noted. That was odd.

Brooks paced as much as the space permitted, basically shuffling in place. "We have to call the police."

"Yeah."

"On the other hand..."

Smith tilted his head. "What?"

Brooks stopped shuffling. "Maybe we ride this thing to our destination and let someone else find it?"

"You're kidding," Smith said.

"I'm not."

"That's devious," Smith said. "But I know you. You're not gonna let someone else get traumatized."

"I don't want to be on this train any longer than I have to. Do you?"

Smith shrugged. "Not really..." He put a hand to his chin.

"What are you thinking?" Brooks asked.

"Three corpses in under a week is a little high, even for us."

"You think it's a message?"

"Couldn't be," Smith said. "They'd have to know we were gonna stay after Lemon's concert and that we were gonna be in this exact train car and that we'd go to the bathroom before anyone else. I'm just saying it's weird to find three dead bodies in the wild."

"It is." Brooks nodded. His annoyance subsided and he decided against traumatizing some other passenger. "I guess we'll call."

"It can wait 'til Stony Brook ," Smith said. "It'll give us some time to snap a few pictures. We'll find a way to lock this head in here, then leave an anonymous tip. Avoid having to hang around and give the cops a statement."

That plan, not involving a protracted stay on the LIRR, was fine by Brooks. When they arrived at their destination, Brooks reluctantly used his strength to finish breaking the already broken privacy glass window on the outside of the car. He hoisted Smith out of the train, then followed. A few people waiting to board saw this display, but they were too dead inside to care.

The detectives dusted themselves off and headed for the station's emergency phone. Brooks kindly informed 9-1-1 of the decapitated head, and they hightailed it down the road. Next Stop: Susie Darkstick's house.

# 9 / SUSIE DARKSTICK, ESQ.

The Darkstick home was neither dark nor made of stick. Brooks and Smith finally found it after a two-mile walk during which they'd dodged two police cruisers heading for the train station. The home was a Stepfordesque tan brick ranch that sat on half an acre of land, with purple shutters and a wide-open purple door. The backyard featured several trees and an herb garden, while a well-kempt flowerbed accented the front. In the driveway was a purple van emblazoned with bright white family stickers—a woman holding a sword and five children, descending from teen on the left to baby on the right. On the far left was some residue where the largest stick figure was once stuck.

"Are you sure this is the right address?" Brooks asked, inspecting the stickers.

Smith sighed out the word "yeah." He scooted around to the side of the van, where a powder pink version of Susie Darkstick's logo covered the rear sliding door.

When they approached the home's white screen door, it swung open before they could ring the bell. An almost-tween named Brayden stood there, his name written across his muddy soccer jersey.

Brooks spoke in the slow, stupid voice people use against children. "Hi. We're looking for—"

The boy shut the door and yelled over his shoulder. "Mooooooommmmm! Clients!"

There was no reply, so he tried again.

"Moooooooooooooom!"

Nothing. Brayden stared out the screen with disconcerting, dead eyes.

Brooks tried to kill the silence. "So... Brayden, is it?"

Smith rolled his eyes.

"Duh," Brayden said. "It's on my shirt."

"Ha!" Smith said.

"Moooooooooooooooooom! Clieeeeeeeents!"

After another silence, Brayden opened the door. "I'll take you to my mom's office."

Brooks and Smith entered a messy living room, made messier by a barrage of iodized salt flying at them. They pawed at the air to keep it away from their eyes. The culprit, a young girl whose soccer jersey identified her as Chartreuse, gave them the all clear.

"They're not ghosts!" she said.

"I don't think mom has any appointments this evening," Brayden said. "She might be doing research or something, though."

The detectives navigated over a pile of toy building blocks and followed Brayden around a corner, where they were pelted with cloves of garlic. One particularly moist clove—that one of the children had been sucking on—hit Brooks in the side of the neck. He wiped at himself in disgust.

"They're not vampires!" said a child too young for a soccer jersey.

"Fuck. How many kids live here?" Smith asked.

"Five, if we're to believe the van," said Brooks.

"And you thought the L-I-double-R was hell."

When they'd maneuvered around enough toys and empty food containers to fill a dungeonmaster's basement, Brooks and Smith arrived at a black, cracked-open door that bore a wrought iron fleur de lis knocker. This was Susie Darkstick's home office, clearly.

Brayden peeked inside. "Moooommmmmm. Clients."

"Send them in," said a husky female voice. "Denny and the ghost can wait."

Brayden leaned in to push the heavy the door open, then walked away. Smith stepped inside, and Brooks followed.

Behind a desk cluttered with paperwork and baby bottles,

Susie Darkstick looked surprisingly put together for someone whose life was an obvious mess. Black leather and
blacker eyeshadow gave her the style she craved. She looked
up, brushed the one red streak in her black hair away from
her face, and began narrating at a tape recorder, her voice
unnaturally deep.

"Two men walk into my office. They're wearing suits. Tall.
They're either detectives like me or government agents coming to start trouble. Only time and conversation will tell."

"Susie Darkstick?" Brooks asked.

"The one and only," she said in her normal voice. Then
she lowered it again for the tape recorder. "I think the men
are lovers."

Brooks and Smith shared a confused glance.

"I'm Arturo Brooks. This is Edward Smith. We're detectives."

"Detective lovers," Susie growled. "Thoughts of government conspiracy can rest for now. But what do they want?
Perhaps I'm getting close to something. Perhaps they're here
to *shut me down*."

Brooks found himself thrown. "Um... we're here to, uh..."

Smith crossed his arms. "What the fuck is your deal,
Darkstick?"

"The blond one is aggressive. I bet he's suffered like I
have," said Susie.

"Stop narrating," Smith snapped.

Susie tapped her recorder's pause button.

"You know there are apps for that?" Smith asked.

"Not my style," Susie snarled.

"And you know garlic doesn't affect vampires, right?"
Brooks asked.

"What? Of course it does." Susie looked to Smith for
agreement.

He shook his head. "It doesn't."

"Did you come all the way out here to interrogate my

methods?" Susie asked. "I have an office in Brooklyn."

"You *what*?" Brooks glared at Smith.

Smith threw his hands up in surrender. "The website didn't say that."

Susie sighed. "My oldest was supposed to update it. I'm in the Piedmont Building, top floor, 10 a.m. to 3 p.m."

Brooks's glare intensified. "*Anyway*. We've heard a lot about you, so we decided to come here and introduce ourselves."

Staring at a set of orange string lights hanging along the wall, Smith didn't even try to cover his lie with enthusiasm. "Yes. We've heard so many great things."

Susie tapped the record button and lowered her voice again. "Word is spreading. Susie Darkstick is a name feared among creatures of the night. Someone will talk. Sooner or later, someone will talk and I'll know what *really* happened to Dev." She hit pause again.

Brooks wondered out loud. "Dev is...?"

"*Was*," Susie corrected. "He was my husband."

"Our condolences," Brooks said. A table in the corner caught his eye. Covered in candles and amulets, it was ripe for an idiot to attempt magic beyond their ability. "You're not trying any black magic, are you?"

"Not anymore," said Susie. "I'm close to finding his killer."

"Anymore?" Smith mumbled.

"His killer?" Brooks asked.

"I'm not sure what it was yet, but I know it was a supernatural being."

"And you know that because...?"

Susie cleared her throat so she could continue to speak in a deep voice. "Detective instinct."

As she spoke, she rubbed at her necklace. Brooks squinted at her, but decided it was nothing. If he hadn't been so fussy about using his cyborg powers, he could have zoomed in and seen its lamp shape. But he was fussy, so his abilities went to waste.

"Are you a lawyer, Darkstick?" Smith asked. He'd been scanning the walls for signs of any credentials whatsoever and seen nothing but a few crappy crayon drawings and Chartreuse's 'No New Cavities' certificate.

"No. Why would you think I'm a lawyer?" Susie asked.

"Your website says *esquire* after your name."

"Oh... no. The Illuminati are esquires. I'm trying to lure them in," Susie said.

Brooks shot Smith a look of exasperation. "Okay. We need to get home."

Smith checked his phone. "Yeah. Long day."

Brooks roped an arm around Smith and moved him toward the door. "Good luck with the Illuminati and your garlic," he said to Susie.

On the detectives' way out, they could hear Susie continue her narration.

"The detectives wish me luck. I doubt their sincerity, but I don't doubt they're on my side. They could prove useful in the struggle to come."

When Brayden had escorted them outside and shut the door, Brooks leaned against Susie's van.

"Okay," Brooks said. "I can live with people leaving our office and going to see an insane woman, but she's on the *top floor* of the Piedmont Building and we're in the basement?"

"Uber's here," Smith said, eyeing a Prius pulling up to the curb.

"We don't have the money for that," Brooks said.

"We'll find the money. I'm not taking you on a train again."

That was Smith's version of being sweet, but Brooks loathed ride-sharing companies—a side effect of being raised by a taxi driver—and he groaned, "You could have at least called a cab."

"If you wanted to wait another hour and pay *even more*, sure—hey now."

The passengers exiting the Prius caught Smith's eye.

"What are you two doing here?" Brooks asked.

"Oh. Hmm." Patience froze.

Lemon bounced up and down. "Patience has a *date*."

"With Susie Darkstick?" Smith asked.

"Who?" Lemon and Patience said at once.

"I'm guessing Darkstick isn't her real name," Brooks said.

"I'm unaware of any Ms. Darkstick," Patience said. "My date is with Kayden Desai."

"Well, you just made our oppo a lot easier," Smith said. He reached for his wallet and pulled out a condom. It was—miraculously—unexpired, and he extended it to Patience. "Here. Take this."

The Puritan turned bright red. Thanks to the Little Achievers Academy's *Abstinence... or Whatever* education plan, she knew exactly what a condom was for. She kept her arm extended as far as it could go to keep the thing away from her.

Brooks slapped himself in the forehead. "Why—"

"If the situation arises, are *you* going to turn down a threesome with Anderson Cooper?"

"No. I was going to ask why you would give that to *Patience*." Brooks yanked the condom away and turned to Lemon. "Just keep an eye on her."

"Yup. That's why I'm here," Lemon said. "You're looking at Lemon Jones, life coach."

"Life coach?" Brooks asked.

"I'm gonna teach Patience how to have a fulfilling life."

"*You* don't have a fulfilling life," Brooks said.

"I know," Lemon said. "It's perfect."

Smith couldn't make any words leave his gaping mouth.

"Have *fun*," Brooks offered.

He and Smith hopped into the backseat of the car and

shared a the-end-is-nigh stare.

# 10 / THURSDAY

Smith was pessimistic about everything, even his own pessimistic outlook. He hated it. More than that, he hated that it was almost always right. His premonition that something bad would happen had become reality... again. Brooks was nowhere to be found.

While Smith was waiting on the steps outside the courthouse for two hours, he began mulling over all the other terrible things that had happened to him and all the terrible things that would inevitably happen to him in the future. Despondent, he slumped, pale and sweaty. Were it not for his suit, he'd have easily been mistaken for one of the homeless denizens sprinkled throughout the area. As he was, more than one passerby judged him a stockbroker on a bad trip.

The end was not nigh. That's what Smith tried to convince himself, but the easily depressed clone could only fake so much. When something bad happens, some people think "worse things have happened" as a means of getting through it. Hey, tougher odds have been overcome, right? What's a little bit of food poisoning compared to your uncle's cancer diagnosis? A little breakup is nothing compared to starving children in X country, you know. That sort of thing.

It wasn't working. For Smith, negative events were additive, and his thoughts spiraled. *He's dead. Everyone's dead and I'm living in a simulation. Or I'm dead again. I'm still dead? Someone's dead. Someone's always dead.*

Brooks had set out earlier in the morning to get patched, just in case he had hidden programming that could, for instance, turn him into a murderbot upon uttering the words "I do." That's what he said, anyway. The two were supposed to reconvene at the courthouse at ten o'clock. It was past noon.

Smith pulled off the ring he'd been wearing and rolled it around in his fingers. His phone was set to full volume, and he scrutinized it. Nothing. Having drunk his own coffee as well as the one he'd brought for Brooks, he desperately had to pee. But he couldn't bring himself to leave the meeting spot. He tried to think himself out of despair.

*This is fine*, he thought. *You're not the one who wanted to get married in the first place. Now it's like he divorced you without the paperwork.*

It didn't help.

*Something awful happened. He's dead.*

That thought didn't help either. He dialed out again. No answer.

"Hey, babe. I'm still here," he said to voicemail. "Hope you're not dead."

*Nothing awful happened. It's me. He's not here because I'm me. Just leave. I should leave.*

Smith's emotional wounds were enough to justify his train of thought. Those aside, the fact was they lived in a world where people could be abducted by monsters and never be seen again. And as visible fighters of those monsters, they were targets. That stint Brooks did as a superhero? It made him famous. Only a year earlier, they couldn't get into their home without pushing their way through a crowd of sign-wielding pro-vampire activists. It was hard enough for Smith to believe Brooks wanted to remarry him, but even if he did...

*He's dead*, Smith thought. *Definitely dead. What the hell am I gonna do now?*

Smith waited two more hours, to no avail, before sulking back to the ADHOC office. He couldn't face Patience's naive remarks or Lemon's incessant questions. He needed to be alone, even if (when) that made matters worse.

*<br>**

At the Piedmont Building, several more hours of sulking and bad thoughts went by. Then a shadow appeared in the doorway, blocking the lone, narrow, slice of hallway light that infiltrated the office. The scratching metallic sound of an old key in an old deadbolt penetrated his woe just in time to catch Brooks entering the room. Thankfully, the key prevented any BLORRRN. Its comedic effect would have been inappropriate, given the circumstances.

Even in indirect hallway light, Brooks looked as awful as Smith felt. His black suit was dusted with a greenish-white film and shredded at the back, his tie dangled sadly from a few threads, and his hair was matted to his forehead.

"I am *so* sorry," he said as soon as he saw Smith.

All of the above made a compelling case for Brooks having had a good reason to miss their second wedding, but Smith was in a mood.

"Yeah. Okay," he grumbled.

Brooks couldn't see Smith's face in the dark corner of the office, but he found his voice worrisome. "Have you been drinking?"

"I wish," Smith said. His tone didn't waver. "It's fine."

Brooks flipped on the lights and found Smith leaned back in his chair, arms crossed, staring at nothing. He appeared totally shell-shocked.

"It's not fine," Brooks said.

"I told you. I *know* you. And when things start to get good they fucking... go bad. It's fine."

"I'm serious. There was a ghoul." Brooks rolled his chair next to Smith and dropped into it. "Check me for ectoplasm."

"I don't care," Smith said. "I told you *I get it.*"

"If you would ju—"

"*I get it.*"

"*Venga!*" Brooks slammed a hand down on the side of Smith's chair. On account of the cyborg strength, the chair arm snapped off and fell to the floor. Brooks cringed a little in embarrassment. Smith cringed a little in concern.

"Stop hating yourself for three seconds and listen to me," Brooks said.

Smith followed the second direction.

"I thought about it, okay?" Brooks said, his face one of obvious shame. "I thought about not marrying you again. But you know I overthink everything. This? This is a crazy misunderstanding."

"A misunderstanding?" Smith asked. "I sat there for *four hours*. You couldn't call?"

"It *ate my phone*." Brooks reached into his back pocket and tossed Smith a half-digested phone, crumpled and sticky with ectoplasm.

Smith inspected it and began cackling.

Brooks continued, "I don't know your new number without it, so I went home. I called you from Patience's phone when I got there, but you never answered. I texted. I emailed."

Smith's cackle softened to a chuckle. "My battery died a while ago."

Brooks continued. "Since you weren't home, I hoped you'd be here. I left a message here too." He gestured at their desk phone, where a blinking red light meant Smith had never checked the message.

"If I wasn't here, where would you have gone next?"

"The morgue?"

"Holy shit, Brooksy."

Brooks smirked. "What, you can't handle dark humor?"

Smith snorted. "An actual misunderstanding... *Jesus Christ*."

Brooks smiled slightly. "I know you're all doom and gloom, but really. It's okay for things to be fine." He tilted his head. "Granted, it's all sort of spiraled out of control since the time machine, but there's no reason we can't have another eight good years." He paused. "Or more. We should aim for more."

"Yeah, well... that time machine fucked me for a lifetime." Smith's pre-clone body had lived to be over a hundred, and very few of those were good years. Time travel had been, was, is, and will continue to be a pain in the ass.

Brooks consoled his partner with a gentle pat. "I know. Let's go home, and we'll go to the courthouse tomorrow morning *together*. If there's a ghoul, nobody gets left behind."

"It's getting late," Smith said. "I was just gonna sleep here."

"It's only a few blocks," Brooks said.

Smith shook his head. "I'm exhausted."

The office chairs bumped against each other as Brooks leaned in to Smith. "Well then I'm staying too." He bounced up out of his chair. "I put an emergency pillow in my desk for just this—"

Smith stood up, grabbed Brooks by the jacket, and pulled him back. Brooks turned and Smith's mouth immediately overtook his. Things tasted a little ectoplasmy, but it didn't seem to matter. They kissed the way people can only when they've just been fighting.

Brooks took a step back. "You are really set on defiling this office, aren't you?"

Smith's tie was already loose, so it took only a moment for him to slide it off. "I'm set on defiling *you*. It doesn't really matter where."

"Seriously? I'm disgusting," Brooks said.

Smith tossed his jacket to the floor. "A little ghoul spunk never hurt anyone."*

"I adore you," Brooks said before diving back into a kiss. He'd normally have refused any kind of contact until he could hit the communal shower, but he'd already let Smith down enough for one day. So kissing it was.

---

* That wasn't true.

Things got explicit from there. You're an adult so you can either live with that or flip ahead to the next chapter. If you're not an adult, your parents are obviously lax, so do whatever you want. Use their credit cards. Get yourself something nice.

It didn't take long for Brooks's dusty suit jacket to join Smith's on the floor. He dropped to his knees, taking Smith's pants with him.

Smith snickered. "I was saving myself for marriage."

Brooks had already gotten started, but removed his mouth just long enough to mumble, "Shut up."

For some time, Smith did. He stood, admiring the view and guiding Brooks's head with a gentle hand. Then he had a change of plans.

"You didn't happen to pack emergency lube with that emergency pillow, did you?"

Brooks looked up with a grin. "I'd have to revoke my gay card if I didn't."

"I didn't get a card," Smith complained.

Brooks scooted to the emergency drawer. While he rifled through it, Smith shook off his last vestiges of clothing. Brooks scooted back toward Smith, lube in hand, and Smith grabbed him by the hand and helped him up off the floor. In seconds, they were kissing again.

Smith ran his arm across the desk, sending some paperwork and a fake aloe plant flying. If Brooks hadn't turned off his cyborg enhancements, he would have received a warning about the desk's weight capacity. As it was, Smith pushed Brooks down on his back and dove between his legs. He worked some magic down there until Brooks made a sound that meant "fuck me already."

Smith obliged. Relations were had. While hips met thrusts, a new shadow appeared in the doorway. There was a KNOCKOCKOCK. It went ignored.

The second KNOCKOCKOCKOCK was more annoying

than the first.

Brooks shouted between breaths, "Come. Back. Tomor-row. Morning!"

KNOCKOCKOCKOCKOCKOCKOCK.

"Fuck *off!*" Smith said.

The shadow in the hallway disappeared, taking its knocks with it. Both men instantly forgot it and went back to the matter at hand. And mouth. Not long after, they made awk-ward noises and crumpled onto the desk in a heap. It bowed in the middle.

Brooks sniffed the air and groaned. "We're gonna have to use the micro-shower."

"*Most* of that is ectoplasm," Smith said. He grabbed the emergency pillow and tossed it into the space between the desk and door. "It can wait."

It wasn't much of a pillow—lumpy and flat—but the two cuddled close to share it.

As he nodded off, Brooks remembered and asked, "Do you think that knock was important?"

"No," Smith said. "Probably another rube who gets their news from ConspiracyWeb. I—"

Brooks was sound asleep, snoring.

"—It doesn't matter." Smith closed his eyes and joined him.

# 11 / DJINN AND TONIC

Minus the second wedding, the courthouse was uneventful. It did, however, take a lot longer than expected, and Brooks rushed back to the office to wipe everything down with bleach wipes and take their 11:30 client while Smith got food.

A weak TAPTAP signaled Brooks to open the door, and a triumphant BLORRRRN announced that Smith had returned bearing lunch.

"You have a key," Brooks noted.

Smith shot pointed glances at the large paper bag of food and the drink carrier in his arms. He deepened his voice and spoke at a measured pace, narrating. "I enter the detectives' office. My husband, unlike Susie's, is alive."

Brooks snickered as Smith set the bag and drinks on the desk.

Smith continued narrating. "He glances in the bag, expecting a gyro. Little does he know, Anastas was closed."

"You know," Brooks said, "I've experienced enough trauma that I shouldn't be laughing, and yet—"

"She was *narrating*. We've all got our brand of crazypills, but she was fucking *narrating*." Smith took his seat and reached into the bag. "What happened to whatshisnuts with the gargoyle thing?"

"It was a regular gargoyle," Brooks said.

Smith rolled his head in annoyance. "Of course it was. What about Darkstick? Anything there?"

Brooks rooted around in the Chinese takeout bag as he rattled off details. "Susanne Caroline Desai, née Miller. Forty-one years old. Bachelor's in Comparative Literature from Hunter College."

"Ouch," said Smith.

"She's been a stay-at-home mom for nearly twenty years.

Husband died of a heart attack, and she lost her damn mind. She wouldn't be a threat to us, except that she's offering her services *for free*."

"Eh, this town's big enough for both... the three of us?"

"Yeah," Brooks said. "This building isn't, though. And it's pretty hard to compete with *free*."

"I guess we'll have to find a way to stand out then," Smith said.

"Like actually solving something?"

"That would be a good start," Smith said. "Also, a catchy slogan."

"Catchy how?" Brooks wondered.

"Hell if I know. I don't do words."

A weird habit of Brooks's was that he liked to eat fortune cookies before his food. While Smith uncovered a particularly pungent order of Mongolian beef, Brooks unwrapped a cookie and cracked it. Smith was about to take his first bite when—

"*Oh my God*," Brooks said.

Because that was roughly the same intensity "Oh my God" that the head in the toilet had garnered, Smith lowered his plastic fork. "What?"

Brooks held the fortune in front of his face like it was a piece of evidence and read its text out loud. "Your cyborg manual won't save you."

Smith frowned. "Someone's playing a prank."

"Open yours," Brooks said.

Smith was reluctant to ruin his lunch with a fortune cookie, but the circumstances seemed to warrant it. He cracked the cookie open and read from it. "You'll wish you were dead again." He scoffed.

Brooks's voice wavered a bit with panic. "There's no way someone could know which one of us would get which cookie."

Because Americans eat too much, Chinese restaurants

vastly overestimate the correct number of fortune cookies for any given order. Thus the two men's eyes went to a third cookie resting on the desk.

"You want to check the extra one, or should I?" Smith asked.

"Let's do it together."

Smith unwrapped the extraneous cookie and extended it toward Brooks. "Count of three?"

Brooks grabbed the other side of the cookie, and they counted together. "1... 2... 3."

CRACKK.

Brooks read aloud, "You'll share a grave like you shared this cookie."

"That's not good," Smith said. "Maybe you were right about the head in the toilet."

"It's definitely a message now," Brooks said.

"All right. Enemies," Smith said.

Brooks rattled off a list. "Immortal Puritans. Former Reticent agents. Former Reticent captives. Former Reticent board members. Vampires. Fake vampires. The Association for the Advancement of Vampire Americans. Wraiths. Steve Buscemi..."

Smith added to it. "All those shitty supervillains you fought with the Bedazzlers. Quidrils. Wights. Half the changelings."

"Three quarters," Brooks corrected.

Smith's eyes widened. "*That many* joined the confederacy?"

Brooks nodded. "Yep."

Smith continued, "Ghouls. Goblins. The Witches' Guild. Sewer Monsters."

"Don't forget the were-pigeon," Brooks said.

Smith groaned. "*The were-pigeon.*"

The two pondered in silence for a moment.

"This doesn't fit any of them, though," Smith said. "They'd have to be psychic or something."

Brooks sighed. "I'll turn on my motion detection until we

figure this out. If someone comes for us while we're sleeping, I'll wake up. Actually, I'll just... enable everything."

"You don't have to do that."

"Yeah, I do." Blue lines pulsed outward from the center of Brooks's eyes as he enabled everything he could remember from the manual, which—because he'd uploaded the digital version to his head—was everything in the manual. "If I don't do everything I can and something happens, I won't be able to forgive myself." He checked his HUD and lightened the mood with a smile. "Your new body's in a lot better shape than the last one."

Smith feigned indignation. "Did you just check my vitals without my consent?" He bit his lip. "There's gotta be something kinky you can do with that."

Brooks stared, expressionless. "Your sperm count is low."

"Guess I won't be getting you pregnant."

Brooks snickered.

"The cookies, though," Smith said. "Is there anyone you've interacted with lately that's—"

KNOCKOCKOCK. The knock at the door seemed annoyed, just like it had the previous night.

"Hold that thought," Brooks said. He tapped the button to let the knocker in.

BLORRRRN. A couple entered the room. If Brooks had checked his paint swatches, he would have noted that the man was a Pantone 58-4 C, and the woman a Pantone 322-7 C. He didn't, though, because that would be a weird thing to do.

"Rhett Conner," the man said, extending a hand to Brooks.

Brooks shook it. "Arturo Brooks."

Rhett was one of those guys who makes handshakes last way too long, and Brooks instantly decided that he didn't like him. When Rhett was done making sure he got the last shake in, he extended the same hand to Smith.

Smith remained seated and half-assed the shake. "Edward

Smith."

Solange reached a hand out, intending to follow the same process, but Rhett interrupted her. "This is my wife, Solange."

She let her hand fall and offered a weak wave instead. "Hi."

Rhett surveyed the room, paying particular attention to the framed photo of the detectives and an open gossip rag sitting on the bookshelf. "Not very professional, are you two?"

"Excuse me?" Brooks asked.

Rhett scowled at the open container of Mongolian beef. "Not very professional at all."

"What do you want, *Rhett*?" Smith asked.

Rhett and Solange took seats.

"I stopped by here last night," Rhett said. "You two were *busy*. I stopped by again this morning and there was a piece of paper that said 'CLOSED' taped to the door."

"Shit happens," Smith said.

Rhett put a hand to his chest and started talking about himself, as he was wont to do. "I always make a point of giving disadvantaged groups my business, but you two aren't making it easy."

Smith, who was still very much white, glanced at Brooks and mouthed, *Disadvantaged?*

Brooks, still annoyed by the handshake, didn't appreciate Rhett's attitude. "You're not doing us a favor by being here. We don't owe you anything. We don't know who you are, and at this point we're probably not taking you as a client."

"I don't want to be a *client*," Rhett said. "I'm trying to solve my own case."

"Your *what*?" Brooks asked.

Solange shot her husband a tepid glance.

"*We*," Rhett said. "Solange and I are working together."

Brooks snapped. "How many paranormal detectives are there now?"

"Did you expect you'd be the only ones?" Rhett asked.

"No, but I didn't think we'd keep running into them," Brooks said.

"You said you were giving us business." Smith ignored his partner and tried to move the conversation with the Conners along. "Why are you here?"

"Oh, we'll pay you if you help. Consider it a consultation. We used to work for the Reticent," Rhett said.

"And?" Brooks asked. Thousands had worked at their former office.

"*And*," Rhett said, "there's a djinn loose somewhere. It was contained at Reticent HQ until *someone* burned that to the ground."

"Not sorry," Brooks said.

"A gin?" Smith asked.

"A *genie*," Rhett said, scowling. "No wonder the company went under with *you two* in charge."

Solange tried to ease the tension with a question. "Have either of you noticed anything strange going on lately?"

"Yeah," Smith said. "We—" Brooks kicked him under the desk, and Smith changed the course of his sentence. "—solve strange shit for a living."

"She means anything especially strange," Rhett said. "Something that can't be explained by ghosts or superhumans maybe?"

"Nothing's ringing a bell," Brooks said.

Rhett handed over a business card—pale nimbus with raised lettering. "If you do, let me know. We need to shove that thing back into a bottle before it causes a disaster."

"We will," Brooks said, accepting the card.

"I'll make it worth your trouble," Rhett said. He got up from his chair and directed Solange to do the same. "Come on."

"Hang on," Brooks said. "Can we talk to her for a second?"

Solange glanced back and forth between her husband and

the detective. "Why?"

Brooks repeated, "*Alone*?"

It wasn't uncommon for the people they interviewed to want to speak to Solange instead of Rhett, on account of his being a douche. Rhett eyed Brooks with suspicion but agreed.

When he was out the door with a BLOOOORNNN, Brooks looked Solange in the eyes. "Is he hurting you?"

"What? No." Her voice conveyed genuine perplexion. "Why would you think that?"

"Because—"

Smith finished Brooks's thought. "Because he's an ass-hole."

"What? No, no. He's just frustrated because we came here three times is all," Solange said. "He can't stand Brooklyn. He says it's full of people who are smug about doing nothing."

"...kay," Brooks said.

"You're sure there's a genie?" Smith asked.

"I don't know if there was or not. I was a researcher." She leaned in close. "Between us, I think if the Reticent had captured a djinn, they would have let me study it. But Rhett... He worked for the Reticent for ten years and all he ever did was paperwork. He never got to see anything paranormal. He's so excited to catch this thing that I don't want to ruin it for him. It's given him a sense of purpose, y'know?"

"...kay," Brooks said.

"You want in on a secret?" Solange asked.

"Not really," said Smith.

She didn't accept that as a serious response and continued. "Djinn can see people coming. So even if it's still out there, I figure it will leave before we can capture it."

"...kay," Brooks said.

"So you're leading your husband on a wild goose chase?" Smith asked.

"It's about the *journey*." Solange turned to leave then glanced back at them with a smile and a wink. "Let us know if you see one."

"We will," Smith said.

BLOOOORN.

"We won't, will we?" Smith said.

"No," Brooks said. "There's something up with that guy. He probably wants to do something super creepy with that genie like start a sex harem."

"I agree, but we do have three corpses and spooky fortune cookies. You think it's a genie?"

"I don't know. I don't know anything about genies," Brooks said. "Do you?"

Smith shook his head. "Just that they're supposed to be an 'oh shit' level event, if they exist."

There had been no 'oh shit' level event described in the Reticent handbook, but genies had been number twelve on a list of forty-three potentially apocalyptic scenarios. If there was a genie in Brooklyn, the detectives—along with everybody else—were in serious trouble. The kind of trouble that required serious research.

# 12 / THE MAKE-A-WISH TEMPTATION

Smith grabbed the remote and turned down the volume.

"I like the Mastiff," he said.

"Are you insane? Did you even see the Chinook?" Brooks asked.

Brooks and Smith's serious research had turned to serious procrastination. While Burroughs and Lemon debated the finer points of concert flyers in the kitchen, the detectives sat on the couch, debating the finer points of a National Dog Show rerun. The genie case came up again only when a certain commercial hit the airwaves.

A frat broish voice shouted over a black screen with pink text. "Paranormal problem? When darkness sticks it to you, darkstick it back. Call Susie Darkstick. 877-GETSTICK. That's 877-GETSTICK." A guitar riff closed the commercial.

"*God,*" Brooks said. "We have to figure out how we're going to advertise."

"What did her husband do that she has this much money?" Smith wondered.

Lemon's pickiness over fonts already had Burroughs ready to fight, and that question sent her over the edge. She called out from the kitchen. "Why do you assume it's *his* money?"

"Oh, hi," Smith said.

"Already did the research," Brooks said. "She was a kept woman."

Smith added, "More money than sense. We can introduce you if you want."

"Yeah, she'll probably be family soon," Lemon said. Patience was out with Kayden for a third time, critiquing a history exhibit on Puritans.

"Not while I can still breathe," Brooks said.

Burroughs acquiesced. "I'll pass."

Smith had a sarcastic idea. "Maybe she *wished for* all the money. From a *genie*."

Brooks giggled.

"A genie?" Burroughs asked. "Did I miss something?"

Smith explained. "Not much. This douchebag who used to work for the Reticent—Rhett Conner—came by asking if we'd seen a genie."

"He called it a djinn," Brooks said. "And we haven't. Obviously."

Smith added, "He was a real dick to us and his wife, so we sent them on their way. We've tried looking into it ourselves, but nada."

That was enough to propel Burroughs out of her chair. Lemon gave her the stink eye as she joined the detectives in the living room. Burroughs loomed over them with a chastising look. "Let me get this straight. There's a trail of corpses everywhere you go..."

"Yes," Brooks and Smith said together.

"...And a guy tells you he's investigating a genie and to let him know if anything strange has been going on..."

"Yes," they said again.

"...And you don't tell him because... what? Just because he's a dick?"

"It's not a pissing contest thing," Smith said.

Burroughs squinted. "It sure sounds like one."

Brooks shook his head. "No. There's something wrong there. I can't find any record of him having ever worked for the Reticent like he said."

"Name change?" Burroughs suggested.

"No. I ran his face against all the old badge ID photos. Nothing."

"Okay," Burroughs said. "Maybe he's just a liar."

Brooks shrugged. "Probably. That's why we're not telling him anything."

Smith leaned back and put his fist to his chin. "I don't think there's a genie."

"Why not?" Burroughs asked.

"Look at the world," Smith said, unclenching his fist and gesturing as if to present the world. "You think anyone's wishes are coming true?"

"Maybe if they're terrible people," Brooks said.

"I don't know." Burroughs rendered an example. "Someone with barely any imagination could have wished for a little bit of money and for their kids to be nice to them. It wouldn't have to be world peace or the biggest fortune on the planet or anything."

"Or it could have been," Brooks said. "Maybe Jeff Bezos found a lamp and—"

"Rubbed one out," Smith said.

"No," Brooks and Burroughs said.

Brooks furrowed his brow. "What if it's Tom Brady?"

Lemon's voice called from the kitchen doorway, only half-aware thanks to Twitter. "You guys have a genie?"

The group shared glances, unsure how to answer that, until Smith answered that. "No one does."

"Someone might," Brooks corrected.

Lemon didn't look up from her phone as she spoke. "Can I have a turn?"

"No," everyone else said.

"No one can have a turn," Brooks said.

"What would you even wish for?" Smith asked.

Lemon looked up and beamed. "Permanent immortality. Uh... fame. And, uh..." She deflated.

"You can't think of a third one?" Brooks asked.

"Well, what would yours be?" Lemon asked.

Brooks thought for a moment. "I don't want to be a cyborg, I want my family alive and well, and... I guess I just want to be content?"

"You're both very selfish," Burroughs said.

Brooks scrunched his face at her. "What would you ask for?"

"World peace, and for Earth to never run out of resources. I'd save the third for when it became clear that I needed it. You know, for an alien invasion or whatever."

"Yeah, I guess that's better..." Brooks trailed off, wallowing in his selfishness.

Lemon looked at Smith. "How about you?"

"I'm not touching that shit," Smith said.

"We all answered," Brooks said.

"No, I mean I wouldn't touch that shit. There has to be some catch."

"Well, yeah," Brooks said. "That's why none of us will be using it. Just hypothetically..."

Smith threw up his hands. "I don't know. Probably something stupid on a whim."

Lemon and Burroughs nodded. Brooks groaned.

"And it doesn't matter," Smith said. "If Solange is right, we'll never find a genie anyway."

"Why?" Burroughs asked.

"Something about if you go looking for them you won't find them."

As they started talking shop, Lemon got bored and buried herself in her phone again.

"I don't think the implication is no one can find a genie," Brooks said. "I think she meant it more like the genie selects who's going to find it."

Smith's eyes lit up. "The wand chooses the wizard?"

Brooks shot him an I-will-murder-you look.

"So, what kind of person would a genie choose?" Burroughs asked.

Smith shrugged. "Beats us. All the texts we've found are written in languages even he can't translate."

"I'm using Google Translate," Brooks said. "Don't make it sound impressive."

"Well, if Google doesn't know the answer, I don't know what to do," Burroughs said without a hint of sarcasm.

Smith nodded.

"Maybe we can find someone who worked in Research and isn't one of the Conners," Brooks said. He, Smith, and Burroughs had been field agents, and they were out of their element. He scanned his records. "Oh. Nevermind."

"What?" Burroughs asked.

"Everyone who worked in Research is dead," Brooks said.

"You sure?" Burroughs asked.

"Yeah. That or they went into witness protection and faked their deaths. Either way, nothing."

"Well, that's shady," Smith said.

"Yeah," Brooks said.

"So, what do we do now?" Burroughs asked.

Lemon looked up and caught her eye.

"I mean, what do *you* do?" Burroughs grimaced. "I need to go back to booking concerts and creating flyers."

Lemon nodded and returned to her tweets.

"What *do* we do now?" Brooks asked.

# 13 / MENTALS

While Google continued having trouble translating ancient tomes as well as current languages, the Brooks-Smith family ran into their own trouble trying to get their insurance discount. Patience and Lemon passed their physicals with flying colors, but almost none of Smith's previous medical records matched his current cloned body. He'd spent an entire day in the hospital getting thirty-seven different exams to create a new baseline. He'd also spent an entire day complaining about that. Brooks's doctor, meanwhile, referred him to a different doctor, who referred him to a software engineer. That software engineer didn't know anything about robotics, and referred him to one who did. That software engineer was on vacation.

Two weeks (and a few errant corpse sightings) later, they were finally given the green light to proceed to mentals. The group strolled into Pleasant Humans, a narrow building that served as a cross between a natural medicine shop and a doctor's office. In the back were the woo-woo therapy room and restroom. In front of that was a small waiting area littered with copies of *Natural Health Monthly*. At the very front were two aisles of 'medicine' that included healing crystals and supplements labeled with FDA warnings that they probably wouldn't work.

A little person manned the register, and he had no interest in the products being sold. He barely looked up from a copy of *Natural Health Monthly* that had a copy of *Actual Science* tucked inside.

"Welcome to Pleasant Humans. Let me know if you need anything," he mumbled.

"Thanks," Brooks said.

"This... is fantastic," Smith said, taking it all in.

A cloud-filled poster on the wall behind the cashier read "Today's Mood Is:" and the velcro arrow underneath was positioned on cerulean, rather than cobalt, magenta, or violet. The soft sounds of Ayne, an Enya cover artist, filled the air, along with sixteen different, clashing incenses. The room's lighting almost exclusively consisted of candles, and its seating consisted of flammable, braided wood chairs with no cushions. Brooks and Smith seated themselves on a wicker loveseat, facing Lemon and Patience who did the same. The purple door at the back of Pleasant Humans read "Vinegret Tolfin, Mind Therapist" and it was vague enough that she wasn't lying about her qualifications.^ A chalkboard to the left of the door detailed the group's options, and flyers on a coffee table offered more information. They picked them up.

"Figure out what you want now," Brooks said, as if Patience and Lemon were children waiting in line for ice cream.

TREATMENT MENU:
Chi Alignment*
Chi Alignment Ultra*
Crystal Waltz
Success Blaster
Incense Inhalation
Five Point Check*
Fear Eliminator*
Gem Therapy*
Couples Gem Therapy*
Peppermint Soak
Success Blaster 5000
Couples Peppermint Soak
Energy Synchronization*
Couples Energy Synchronization*

---

^ She had none.

Therapist's Choice

All treatments last 30 minutes. Items marked with an asterisk (*) are ACA-certified mental health treatments.

"I'm gonna go for the crystal waltz," Lemon said.

"You have to do one of the ones with an asterisk," Brooks said.

"Fiiiine," Lemon sighed. "I'll do the chi alignment *ultra*."

Patience frowned. "I don't wish to participate."

Smith laughed. "Sounds like you need the *Fear Eliminator*."

She didn't register his tone as sarcastic. "If you insist."

Smith shook that off and turned to Brooks. "Couples gem therapy or couples energy sync?"

"It's all nonsense, so... your call?"

"The second one sounds like a Vulcan mind meld," Smith said.

Brooks stared through him. "I'll assume that means you want to do that one?"

"Yes."

A floral clock above the purple door ticked 10:29:59 and the door opened. A dreadlocked hippie emerged, holding a plastic baggie of amber marbles.

"10:30. You're up!" the cashier shouted from the front of the store.

Vinegret spoke well before Lemon could see her.

"What ails you, dear?" asked a soft voice without a face.

Lemon glanced around the room. There was no lighting fixture above her. There were no lighting fixtures anywhere, and that itself was concerning. Candles had been banned on Luna in 2152 after one's open flame partnered with a small design flaw to explode three years' worth of food stores.

While she'd gotten used to seeing a votive here and a cande-labra there, she'd never seen anything like the massive altar of lit candles in Vinegret's office. Nor had she smelled any-thing like it. Scents of lavender, fennel, patchouli, oak, and watermelon contrasted horribly to make the place smell like the clearance rack at a bath and body shop.

"I'm fine," Lemon said. She tilted her head, trying to spot the therapist.

A woman in her early sixties popped out from behind a wall. Grey hair, oversized spectacles, and a floor-length BoHo dress conveyed harmlessness, and her sweet voice did the same.

"Are you sure, Lemon?" she asked.

"I didn't tell you my name," Lemon said, taking a step back. She put her arms up, ready to guard herself and punch an elderly woman, if necessary.

"You had an appointment, dear."

"Oh." Lemon relaxed. "I'm gonna get the—"

Vinegret walked toward her. "The Chi Alignment Ultra. I know."

Lemon took another step back and tensed up. "I didn't tell you that either."

Vinegret held up her tablet, displaying a message from someone named Leon:

next one wants the CAU

"The cashier?" Lemon asked.

"He has wonderful hearing," Vinegret said. She sat down in a wicker chair and gestured for Lemon to do the same. "You seem stressed."

"I'm from the future," Lemon said, taking a seat.

Vinegret didn't bat an eyelash. "That must be frustrating."

"Yeah. It is. And my dads are a couple of glorbdinks who don't get it."

"I think chi alignment is a wise choice for you, Lemon."

Lemon squinted. "Why?"

"Frustration is a symptom that you're not living a life that's true to your spiritual self."

"That sounds fake," Lemon said.

"Close your eyes," Vinegret said.

Lemon closed her eyes and rolled them where the woo-woo therapist couldn't see. Then there was a twenty-six minute chant. A low, set of humming noises, it didn't sound like any Earthly or moonly language, but Lemon wasn't a linguist so she didn't take note. Instead, she fell half-asleep.

"All done," Vinegret said.

Lemon jerked awake and nearly fell forward off the chair.

Nothing had happened.

The 11:00 appointment belonged to Patience, who brushed by Lemon on her way in.

Patience flinched. "Is it safe?"

Lemon rolled her eyes. "A safe waste of time." She unironically pulled out her phone to tweet about it.

Patience shuffled inside and seated herself.

"What ails you, dear?" Vinegret asked.

"I was told I must come here so misters Brooks and Smith can get an insurance discount."

"You selected the Fear Eliminator. What do you fear?"

Patience tilted her head in thought. "Dolls."

"Dolls?" Vinegret asked.

Patience nodded. "I believe they contain cast-out spirits."

Vinegret couldn't work with that. "Is there anything else?"

"Burning at the stake. Dancing. Debauchery. Subway trains. Cars. Incurable plagues. Heavy wind. The internet. Courting. Childbirth. Marital relations. The American West. Ancient aliens. Hip hop..."

"Okay, I get the picture."

"Photography as well," Patience said. She couldn't believe she'd almost forgotten that one.

"You poor dear," Vinegret said. "Close your eyes."

Patience frowned. "Must I?"

"It won't work if you don't," Vinegret said.

Patience scanned the room, shut her eyes, and added Vinegret's low mumbling and humming to the list of things she was afraid of. When her time was up, she lifted her dress off the ground and scurried out of the room. Two overly enthusiastic fathers greeted her.

"Our turn!" Brooks said, practically jumping from the wicker.

He didn't want the woo-woo therapy as much as he wanted to escape the Conners. To his chagrin, Rhett and Solange had arrived early for their noon appointment. Apparently the visit was Solange's idea, and watching Rhett be a condescending douche to his wife for half an hour was too much to bear. They were midway through one of Rhett's rants—it was about separating recyclables—when Patience emerged.

Smith hopped up from the chair and waved at Rhett. "Yeah, look at that. We have to go."

"How was it?" Brooks asked Patience.

Patience glanced around, still afraid of the waiting room. "It seems nothing happened."

"Perfect. Wait here."

Patience took her seat, and Rhett stared at her.

"Do you separate your recyclables?" he asked.

Armed with Patience and Lemon's reports of the woo-woo therapy being a bust, Brooks and Smith entered Vinegret's office sharing a smug look.

"Go ahead and have a seat, dears."

Smith made himself comfortable at the corner of the wicker loveseat, his arm stretched out across its back. Brooks sat next to him, leaning slightly into his chest. They appeared content, and not at all like a couple who needed woo-woo treatment.

Vinegret eyed them from her own wicker. "So why do you want the energy synchronization?"

"For the Obamacare discount," Smith said.

Brooks nodded. "Yeah. That."

Vinegret lowered her head. "No other reason?"

"Nope," Brooks and Smith said at once.

"There's nothing the two of you aren't on the same page about?" Vinegret asked.

"Nope," Smith said.

"Well—" Brooks said at the same time.

Smith gave his husband the stink eye and retracted his arm. "Oh, come on."

"There's something then?" Vinegret asked.

"Don't buy in," Smith said. "Don't buy in."

Brooks bought in. "I want another kid. He doesn't."

"That seems like an issue to me," Vinegret said.

"He won't even agree to get a dog," Brooks added.

Smith muttered something about betrayal under his breath.

"I didn't catch that," Vinegret said, "but I think the energy sync will be good for you."

Smith rolled his eyes. "Yeah, whatever. I'd save your best woo-woo for the next appointment."

"What?" Vinegret asked.

"Oh, the Conners. You'll see."

Vinegret's right eye twitched ever so slightly, not enough for the detectives to notice. "Prepare for an experience unlike any other."

Brooks whispered to Smith. "I really want her to meet Susie Darkstick..."

Smith chuckled.

"I'm going to connect your minds, dears," Vinegret said. "I recommend fourteen sessions to fully strengthen the bond between—"

"Yeah, that's great," Smith said, "but we only need one to get the discount, so..."

Vinegret scowled. "I see."

"Yeah, if you could just give us the 'Best Of' today, that would be great," Brooks said.

"Empathic symbiosis is not for the faint of heart," Vinegret said. "We can't possibly cover everything in one session—"

"We have both literally died," Brooks said.

Smith nodded. "I'm sure your woo-woo is intense for Johnny Normal, but he's a cyborg and I'm a clone, so let's get this show on the road."

"If you say so," Vinegret said.

She handed each of them a clipboard with a waiver.

I, _____, agree that Vinegret Tolfin is not responsible (morally, legally, or otherwise) for any adverse reaction to this treatment. While the therapist believes this will be life-changing, I understand that I will be subjected to treatment that has not been proven beneficial in any peer-reviewed studies, and that is illegal in Vermont. I agree that I will not travel to Vermont in the next six months. I am of mostly sound mind and have read the relevant brochure(s).

They signed without reading any brochures.

Vinegret turned the lights down low. "If there's anything at all you don't want to share with each other, think about it right now."

Brooks and Smith exchanged an eyeroll, but Smith quickly thought of something. Vinegret gave him a conspiratorial wink.

"Now. Hold hands," she said.

They did.

"Gaze into each other's eyes."

They did.

"Focus on each other's energy."

They had no idea what that meant. Not even Brooks, with his cyborg bits enabled.

Vinegret began her signature mumble-chant. Out of nowhere, she broke cadence and shouted a non-word.

"Krekor!"

"Did she just say 'crack whor—'" Smith's question was cut off by searing pain at his temples, and in his agony he asked another. "What the fuck?"

"I take it your husband gets migraines," Vinegret said.

"He used to before the cyborgening," Smith said. He pressed his temples, trying to make it go away. "This is what that feels like? Fuck."

Within seconds, Smith remembered the aforementioned cyborgening—something Brooks had been programmed to forget. Pain far worse than a migraine. His eyes being ripped out and replaced with high-tech sensors. A surgical drill boring into the base of his spine. "Ow. Fuck." He felt memories being ripped from his mind and replaced with evil Puritan programming. The horror of not being able to figure out what was missing. Then more cutting. More drilling. The installation of a precarious USB port.

"I wanna go back to Kansas..."

The pain gave way to other feelings new to Smith. Pure contentment. Familial love. Those were more a stranger to him than the torture. He remembered Christmases with Brooks's family as if they were his own. He felt the pain that Brooks had felt watching his family die, and the love Brooks had for him and the girls that filled that void. Most striking was the intensity of Brooks's feelings. How good something as simple as a smile could make Brooks feel.

Love was dialed up to eleven, but so was hatred. Brooks

had a lot of it, for everything that prevented him from having a normal life. He hated the Reticent doctors who operated on him, the wraiths that murdered his family, Godwin Zane. On top of the loathing, there were revenge fantasies that Smith could never have the passion to imagine. Brooks wanted those who'd hurt him to suffer. Painfully. Staking vampires wasn't a duty; it was a pleasure. Decapitating demons was doubly so. The thought of slowly choking Godwin Zane to death was practically orgasmic.

Smith's voice faltered. "I... don't like woo-woo therapy."

Brooks, meanwhile, fell completely silent. In place of his own memories, he had Smith's. Each painful moment beating him down more and more, until there was barely a person left. Brooks's eyes went still and glassy, and his hands shook enough that even Vinegret (who was not a detective) noticed.

"I think you should let go of him," she said.

Smith obliged.

Brooks buried his head in his hands and clawed at his hair. He whimpered something unintelligible and nearly fell off the seat. He followed that up with a long sound that was half groan, half shout.

Smith rescued him with an extended arm and turned to Vinegret. "What the hell did you do?"

"I gave you fourteen sessions worth, like you asked."

"Well *I'm* not having a total meltdown," Smith said.

"Different people handle pain differently," Vinegret said.

Brooks choked through tears. "Everything is awful."

"Fuck," Smith said again.

"If you'd like, I could get the crystals of intent—"

Smith cut her off. "Can you just leave us alone for a minute?"

Vinegret scoffed, "You have six minutes until time runs out. I'll go make more purified sand."

Smith still felt like his eyes were being torn out, but he pressed onward. "Babe, talk to me."

Brooks pulled at his arms, almost like he was trying to remove his own skin. His face shimmered with sweat. "Everything is awful."

"I know," Smith said.

"All of your memories. All of them. At once."

It struck Smith as odd to console someone for experiencing his own life, but he pulled Brooks closer. "It's okay."

Brooks pulled back. "It's not okay. It's one awful thing after another. I have no idea how you function."

"Not well," Smith said. "You might have noticed."

Brooks's eyes transitioned to a cold, alert gaze. "I wish I could kill everyone who ever hurt you."

"Okay, that's a little psychotic," Smith said, the revenge fantasies still fresh in his mind.

"I mean it," Brooks said.

"No, you don't," Smith said. "You're all fucked up on empathic woo-woo."

"I never knew most—"

"Yeah, and I'm not gonna talk about any of it," Smith said. He glowered at Vinegret. "When does this wear off?"

Vinegret looked up from her bucket of sand and gave an answer that was far too chipper. "Never. The emotional response will pass, but the memories will be with you forever. The energy synchronization is—"

"Awesome," Smith groaned.

"Thank you," Vinegret said. "I think so."

Smith stood to leave and helped Brooks do the same. Brooks wobbled a little, and Smith's arm went around his waist to keep him steady. They said nothing more to Vinegret, preferring to let their glowering speak for itself.

On their way out, they brushed by the Conners.

"How did it go?" Rhett asked.

Brooks mumbled a little.

"What?" Rhett asked.

"Get the energy sync," Smith said. "It's *great*."

# 14 / WAKE UP CALL

Another day of clients passed. They were good for breaking up the silence at ADHOC, but little else. One man had been convinced he saw a monster. It was a hippopotamus, and he was at the Bronx Zoo. His was the most plausible paranormal report of the day. The least plausible was the case of the haunted notebook paper. After an hour staring at a sheet of paper and waiting for it to move on its own, Brooks and Smith realized their client had previously turned on a box fan. The client, in turn, realized he had no reason to pay the detectives and walked out, stiffing them.

Smith was berating him on the phone. "Yeah, it's nothing... You should pay us because you wasted our time on nothing... Do you remember signing a contract?... Just fucking... No, I won't apologize for swearing. Fuckity fuck fuck fuck. Pay us." He wiggled the phone at his ear. "Hello?"

Brooks shut his laptop. "Let's just go home."

"It's only two," Smith said.

"Do you see any reason to stay?"

Smith didn't. Aside from the worthless clients, no one knew anything about genies. What little was translatable was myth or speculation, and the detectives were still stuck. But now they were stuck and broke and annoyed that they'd had their brains messed with by a woo-woo doctor. After just five hours at the office, they gathered their coats and headed out to make the short walk home.

"You okay?" Smith asked. "You've been quiet all day."

"I'm fine. Annoyed at the paper guy, but fine. Vinegret was right about whatever that was wearing off. I don't feel your memories anymore. Now it's more like I just... know facts? Are you sure you're okay?"

"No, same as usual." Smith squinted. "Why? Did I do

something weird?"

"No, but..."

"But *what?*" Smith spoke like he was ready for confrontation.

Brooks sighed. "We're not going to talk about this?"

"Nope," Smith said.

"It was horrible, and I just—"

"Stop." Smith shot him a stern look. "*My* memories aren't *your* problem. Pretend it never happened."

Brooks sighed in exasperation. "I can't do that."

"Sure you can. Just like I can pretend I don't remember you banging a bunch of old dudes." It wasn't the most concerning part of Brooks's memories by a long shot, but Smith wanted to keep things light.

"They weren't *that* old," Brooks complained.

Smith stared, unblinking.

"Okay, they were kind of old," Brooks said.

"I know. I was there." Smith tilted his head. "Sort of."

As they neared the brownstone, Brooks came to a stop. "Seriously, Eddie. I can't pretend I don't remember your whole life now."

Smith, who had been a few paces ahead, stopped and turned around. "Why?"

"Because I care about you. And because so much makes sense now. Even down to your poor dog—"

"I know it sucked. I was there." Smith stepped in close, his eyes telling Brooks to drop it. "You think if we have a special share time I'll feel better?"

Brooks was a big believer in talk. "Maybe."

Their voices had gotten loud enough that a passerby crossed the street so she wouldn't have to walk near them.

"Try this," Smith said. "If you remember my entire life, then you know I've talked about this shit before. No one needs it. All it does is drive people away."

Brooks curled his lip. "You haven't talked about it to me."

"It doesn't matter." Smith said.

"It does matter."

Smith switched his annoyed voice to a dreamier one, like a self-help audiobook narrator or someone teaching painting on public broadcasting. He wrapped his arms around himself in a fake hug. "We'll have some tea and a nice cry, and then you'll get a tingly feeling knowing you're the kind of guy who can make problems disappear into thin air."

"Problems don't disappear, and that's not what I'm trying to do," Brooks said. "It's cold. You're irritable. Let's just go inside."

"Fine."

Smith entered first and hung his coat. He was already cold, but now he froze. Something was amiss, and not in a fun way. The TV was off, Lemon's silenced phone was abandoned on an end table, and the entire house smelled like cookies.

Patience scurried over. "Welcome home, sirs."

Lemon waved from the kitchen. "Hey! Cookies are almost done!"

Smith looked back to where Brooks was shutting the front door. "What did you tell them?"

"Nothing," Brooks said.

That was bullshit, and Smith recognized it as such.

"Bullshit," he said.

Patience lowered her head.

"See?" Smith said. "Bullshit."

Brooks gave a sad smile. "I just thought we could all stand to be nicer to—"

"Oh. Okay." Smith's face reddened. "You wanna know why I keep things private? This."

"What? So people won't be nice to you?" Brooks asked.

Smith raised his voice. "I don't need to be treated like a delicate... thing that's delicate."

"I'm just trying to—"

"I know what you're trying to do." Smith used his hands to declare dinner a wash. "I'm out." He reached for his still-chilly coat and put it back on.

"Eddie—"

"*No.* Once again, therapy has fucked me over."

"Hey, it wasn't exactly great for me either," Brooks said.

"It was *your idea.*" He imitated Brooks's voice. "We'll get the woo-woo, it'll be fun."

"We both agreed to get the discount."

"Whatever," Smith said.

Brooks stayed between him and the doors, arms folded. "What are you doing?"

Smith brushed him aside. "Going for a walk."

"You don't go for walks."

"And Lemon doesn't bake cookies. We're all trying new things!"

Smith huffed aimlessly down a street, kicking stray pieces of trash along the way. It was damn cold, and his breath was visible in the air. He considered that a few drinks would warm him right up, but decided that—no—he wasn't quite that angry. He'd gone three miles and wasn't angry at all, really. Brooks's heart was in the right place, and there's no way he'd told the girls anything deeply personal. Smith felt better, which made him feel like shit.

*You're such an asshole*, he thought. *Maybe next time go for a walk before snapping at your husband for being nice to you.* Then his mind betrayed him. *Just die, you fucking idiot. Oh, fuck. I really do need therapy.*

Instead of hating himself, Smith should have been minding his surroundings. He'd wandered pretty far in the wrong direction, into a neighborhood best described by the sound 'oof.' A larger, fitter man walked toward him, carrying himself the way people itching to start fights do. As they passed each other, the brute rammed a shoulder into Smith, sending him tumbling into an alley. Smith went down and caught himself with his hands, which broke through a thin layer of ice and landed in a grey puddle with a SPLASH. The man towered over him.

"What the fuck?" Smith asked. He rose to one knee and clutched a painful wrist.

In a quick motion, there was a gun pointed at his face.

"Wallet. Phone. Watch," the man said.

"Who the fuck wears a watch?" Smith asked.

His lack of any self-preservation instinct was stunning. Smith's response was a poor one, and the mugger's answer to it was a bullet. He shot away from Smith. It was meant to be a warning—just something to frighten him into ditching the sarcasm—but the bullet ricocheted off a brick wall and hit Smith in the cheek. It ripped through his face before he realized what had happened. Tooth shards and blood filled his mouth, and he instinctively dropped back to the ground, clutching the sides of his face.

"Shit," the mugger said with a casual tone.

Before Smith could fully process the pain, he thought, *Who gets shot in the face?* Once he could process it, he thought, *Fuck*.

While blood poured out from between his lips, Smith's tongue probed the side of his mouth and found a large chunk of flesh barely hanging on to the side of his face. Touching it loosened it. The piece dropped down into the back of his mouth and Smith gagged.

*Fuuuuuuuuck.*

His attacker gave him a quick pat-down in search of a watch and cell phone, realized there weren't any, and made do with just the wallet. Since he'd accidentally shot his victim once, he decided to do it again and keep him silent. Two quick shots to the chest, and he ran off.

Smith collapsed to the ground, face down and bleeding.

There were distant sirens, but there were always distant sirens and there was no way of knowing whether they were coming to render help. It seemed hopeless. He was cold from the lost blood, but hot where its warmth poured out of him. Everything felt tight, and he doubted he could move enough to do what he needed to do.

The mugger's rushed search was a blessing. Smith choked out an agonized groan as he struggled to unzip an inner coat pocket and take out his cell phone. He was definitely going to die, and it was important to him that Brooks not blame himself. He wasn't sure he could breathe, let alone speak, but he had to try. He couldn't let their last conversation be a fight. Especially not a fight over Brooks trying to be nice. There were cookies, for fuck's sake.

*Come on. Answer*, Smith thought between *Oww* and *Fuck*. He didn't have enough limbs to press at all of his wounds, so he let the pavement do the job on his chest. Gravel was definitely working its way into his wounds, but he worked with what he had. Lying flat on his stomach, he slid the phone up to his face and managed three taps: Contacts > Brooksy > Speaker.

Smith brought his hands back to his face, pressing at the holes on either side.

"Hey," Brooks said, ready to make amends.

Smith's body wanted him to scream, "Help me." Everything was burning, especially his lungs, and his labored breaths made it apparent that something was wrong.

"Eddie? Are you okay?" Brooks said.

Smith slurred a response. "I... I... fug... up..."

"Are you drunk?" Brooks asked.

"No... shot..."

"You did shots?" Brooks got pissy. "Great."

"No... got... shot..."

The sidewalk in front of Smith turned fuzzy, and he could no longer read Brooks's name on his phone. The pain seemed to lessen, like it was something he knew rather than experienced, and the knowledge was fading. He was half in the world and half not, and he knew from experience what came next.

Brooks's voice took a panicked tone. "Where are you?"

"Du... no..."

"Eddie?" Brooks's voice got louder. "Seriously, where are you? I'll come pick you up."

His vision faded completely and his voice was going with it, but Smith got the important words out. "Lub you... kay?" The rest of what he said was unintelligible, but what he intended to say was: "I wish things were different."

# 15 / IF WISHES WERE FORCES

Three months later, Pop Tart & the Activation Energy commemorated Smith's shooting at Madison Square Garden before twenty thousand adoring fans. Gone were the days of dive bars with flickering lights. Their stage was a nonstop spectacle of smoke and lasers, manned by the finest A/V crew around. Having just introduced all the other members of the band, Trevor Tarte moved on to its most popular (after him, of course).

"On lead fiddle... Lemon Jones!"

The crowd went wild as Lemon started a slightly off-key violin solo.

"Three months ago, one of Lemon's dads got shot in an alley," Trevor said.

Low, consolatory sounds came from the stands.

"He's fine! He's fine!" Trevor said. "But that event inspired this next song, and you can—"

The crowd knew which song was coming, and they drowned him out with cheers. It was *the* song. The one that skyrocketed to number one on every chart in America and a few charts overseas. Lemon's violining switched to the score of that song—a quick, frenzied pizzicato—and the audience broke into feverish screams. It was the strongest positive reaction any group of people had ever had to a violin solo.

Trevor moved his hands up and down to calm the crowd. "You can—"

They kept screaming, but the screams softened.

It was good enough for him to finish his sentence. "You can sing along if you know the words!"

Everyone did.

*Take me to the alley*
*Shoot me in the face*
*Watch me walk it off, and*
*Quicken up my pace...*

At the ADHOC office, Burroughs watched the concert livestream on the fifty-inch television in the small but well-equipped break room. She looked away from the screen at Smith. "Does that bother you?"

"That Lemon got her big break writing about me being shot in the face?" he asked.

"Yes, that," Burroughs said. She finished the last bite of her sandwich—another late dinner at the office—and dumped her trash.

"No," Smith said, doing likewise. "Worse things have happened, and... I hate to say it because it's a jinx, but everything has been pretty great since then."

"You've *never* used the word 'great,'" Burroughs said. She extended two fingers to his forehead, pretending to take his temperature. "Are you sick?"

Smith glowered. "Don't you have work to do?"

"Ugh. Yes." She was swamped, in fact. "I *almost* wish I'd stayed with the band."

"They're doing better without you," Smith noted.

"Thanks, Eddie."

He shrugged. "Hey, we're doing better *with* you."

She offered a fake, exaggerated smile.

The three-month uptick in paranormal activity showed no signs of slowing, and ADHOC's twenty-seven employees—occupying the entirety of the Piedmont Building—had as much work to do as the Darkstick Agency's hundred. ADHOC was overburdened on purpose. Taking on more cases and solving them effectively was their key to good word of mouth and even more success. Only when they got to Susie's level—an office in lower Manhattan and adverts on the sides of buses—would they know they'd really made it.

For that reason, Smith felt a little guilty about his next words. "I need to get home."

"It's eight thirty," Burroughs said. "Go."

"You sure?"

"Owen, Trazi, and I can handle the imps, and the faerie-mancer can wait until morning."

"Thanks," Smith said. "I owe you one."

"You owe me six right now," Burroughs said.

Smith froze. "We don't have that kind of relationship anymo—"

"*Six*," Burroughs repeated. "*Six.*"

Back home, Smith hung his coat and took a look around the living room. He didn't stomp this time, opting instead to gently remove his boots. There was no sign of anyone but Widget, the Norfolk terrier who bounded down the stairs to greet him. Smith gave the dog a quick head rub.

"Where's Brooksy?" Smith asked.

Widget didn't answer because he was a dog.

The faint sound of an upstairs TV answered for him: Brooks had already retired to bed. He wasn't asleep—he wasn't *that* old yet—but he was exhausted.

Smith trudged upstairs, went through the door, and began shedding his clothing. He shut the door to keep Widget out, just in case things were about to get sexy. The dog whimpered a little, but got over it and walked away.

Brooks looked up from the bed and smiled. "Hey."

"Sorry I'm late," Smith said.

"Oh, I'll be late tomorrow," Brooks said. "That's life."

Smith, down to boxers and t-shirt, hopped into bed next to him and offered a quick nuzzle. "Need help with anything?"

"Nope," Brooks said. He immediately contradicted himself with a hesitant "I'm... good..."

"That's not convincing," Smith said. "What's wrong?"

Smith couldn't get Brooks to meet his eyes and answer. The bedroom TV was meant to be background noise, but something on it had caught Brooks's attention and he zoned out.

"Just..." Brooks trailed off.

"Tonight on Old TV, it's back-to-back *The Madisons* at ten, followed by *Jolly Days* and *Gilligan's Butte*. For you night owls, *Mork & Mandy* starts at midnight, followed by *Houston*."

Brooks groaned.

"Yeah, we should cancel cable," Smith said. "Everyone's doing it."

"Totally, but that's not it." They weren't supposed to talk shop at home—not anymore—but Brooks couldn't help but let a nagging concern interrupt what should have been cuddling. He pulled away from Smith and made a squinting, confused face. "Something's bothering me."

"What?" Smith asked, certain it was something he'd done.

Brooks sighed. "It's nothing."

This time, Smith made the squinting, confused face. "Something is nothing?"

"It's nothing specific. I just can't shake the feeling that something's wrong," Brooks said.

"Wrong how?" Smith asked.

"I don't know," Brooks admitted. He couldn't explain it, but in the previous twenty-four hours there was a nagging feeling in his brain, similar to the feeling of leaving an eight-year-old at home alone while the rest of the family travels to Paris.

Smith shook his head. "Christ. You sound like me."

"No. I don't mean it's something *bad*," Brooks said. "I just feel like the world is... off. It's like I'm on drugs or something."

"Well, have you been hitting the crack pipe lately?"

Brooks smacked his shoulder. "No."

"Peyote? Shrooms?" Smith pondered wistfully.

"Eddie. No."

"Things have changed in the past few months," Smith said. "You mean that?"

"No, I know it's been eventful. It's not stress. Just... off. Or maybe I'm misremembering things. Like... did Gilligan always have a butte?"

"He did," Smith laughed. He sang along to the theme song. *"With Gilligan, Prospector too, the Mining Chief, and his wife, the two farmhands, and a prostitute... here on Gilligan's Butte!"*

Brooks scratched at the side of his face. "That just... doesn't seem right. How'd they get away with having a prostitute on their show in the sixties?"

"It was ahead of its time," Smith said. "Maybe you need another patch or something."

"I just had one yesterday, but maybe. I don't know..." Brooks said.

Smith sat up straight and forced some cheer into his voice. "I know something."

"What?" Brooks asked.

Smith leaned in and kissed Brooks's neck in a trail that led to his ear. He lingered for some time, alternating soft flicks and gentle nibbles. Ever since that conversation with Burroughs, Smith had six on his mind.

Brooks smiled. "Those aren't words."

"Eh, who needs 'em?" Smith's sentence ended in an abrupt kiss.

That turned into more kissing, which turned into something more explicit. Underpants were removed. Things were tugged. No sooner than Brooks got his mouth exactly where he wanted it, there was an awful scream from the next room. Maria was hungry, filthy, angry, or a combination.

Brooks let out a heavy sigh.

Smith, stripped of excitement, reached for his pajama pants.

"I'll take care of it," he said.

"You sure?" Brooks asked.

"Yeah," Smith said. "You were here all day. Just don't fall asleep."

Smith had never fancied himself a baby person. He still didn't, on account of all the screaming and fluids. But for reasons no one could figure out, Maria took to him more than to anyone else. It only took ten minutes or so to calm the infant, and Smith returned with a triumphant look on his face. Unfortunately, no one was able to see it. Brooks had pulled every last one of their blankets over himself and was fast asleep.

Smith wasn't mad. He settled onto the bed and pulled what little cover he could grab without disturbing Brooks. There might have been a sweet moment if Smith weren't Smith. As he was, he reached down to take care of himself. No sooner than he was about to climax, the screams next door returned.

# 16 / BABY FEVER

The next time Maria started crying, Smith was balls-deep in Brooks. There's certainly a more polite way of phrasing that, but this isn't that story. He deflated and sank to the bed.

Brooks turned around. "Ugh. Just finish."

"I can't," Smith complained. "There is no greater mood killer." He had never heard Jaxx Onomy's solo album *Jaxx of Life*.

"I've got it!" Lemon shouted from the hall. In town for two nights only, she knew what they were up to, and she wanted to help.*

"She's got it," Brooks said.

"Too late," Smith said, looking down with a frown.

"You sure?" Brooks ran a hand up his chest and over his shoulder.

Because Lemon had begun singing to her, Maria screamed even louder than before.

Smith grimaced. "I'm sure."

Brooks sighed and slumped. Smith tucked in next to him and reached for a remote to drown out both Maria's crying and Lemon's vocals. These days, their home lives were about eighty percent sitting around watching TV. The other twenty percent consisted of eating, sleeping, and failed attempts at sex.

On screen, black and white panning shots revealed tight-abbed men and women in white underwear lounging around on uncomfortable futuristic furniture.

"Aspiration," whispered a sultry female voice.

"Aspiration," repeated another.

More underwear-clad models stared directly into the

---

* Abstractly, you pervert.

camera, their cheeks sunken from years of disordered eating. A slow drumbeat became louder.

"Aspiration."

The drums and voices disappeared in an instant, and a silent shot of a lake overtook the screen. It faded to black, and words appeared onscreen in a classy serif font at the same moment they were spoken:

"Aspiration by Rhett Conner."

Brooks groaned. *"That guy."*

"Yeah..."

"I will *never* get how he's so successful," Brooks said.

"Because he's a douche," Smith said. "Successful people are douchebags. Think about the late Godwin Zane."

Brooks glared at him. "I'd rather not."

The next commercial touted another Rhett Conner enterprise. An elderly man dropped his keys and knelt down to pick them up. Everything went slow motion, all color disappeared from the frame, and there was a screeching sound as the man clutched at his lower back.

An authoritative male voice spoke. "Imagine not having to deal with back pain."

A hard-working woman with a frazzled bun flicked off a desk lamp and rubbed at her temples. Everything slowed, greyed, and screeched again.

"Imagine not getting headaches," the voice said.

The visual changed to a group of middle-aged and multicultural adults playing frisbee in a park.

"Imagine total health is within your grasp. Ask your doctor about Imagin."

While more healthy, multicultural adults swam and frolicked on a beach, the voiceover switched to a low, female voice. "Imagin may or may not be right for you. Side effects of Imagin may include: delusions, hallucinations, unjustified hope in the future, addiction to snack cakes, and others. Do not take Imagin if you are pregnant or may become pregnant.

Do not take Imagin if you are cybernetically enhanced. Imagin has not yet been evaluated by the FDA."

"Maybe we should quit being detectives and start selling pharmaceuticals," Brooks said.

"Do you think we're gonna luck into billions like Rhett did to get off the ground?"

"Probably not," Brooks sighed. He was just a little bitter about Rhett finding a dragon and stealing its centuries' worth of treasure.

"Besides, you wouldn't be able to quit," Smith said. "Not with all these fucking cases."

Brooks's eyes lit up.* "That's another thing that's off."

"What?" Smith asked.

"You don't think it's weird that almost nothing happened for years, and now we're swamped?"

Smith squinted. "No? There are people with superpowers, so people become witches and faeriemancers and shit to deal with it. Then they piss off the ghosts and imps and were-wolves and you've got a big fucking mess."

"Yeah, I guess," Brooks said. Something still didn't sit right.

Smith tousled Brooks's hair. "You know what I think? I think you're running on zero sleep, zero sex, and nothing but takeout. We should go on vacation."

"We can't take a vacation," Brooks said. "You just said everything's a mess."

"It's always been a mess. It's always gonna be a mess."

"That's the optimist I love," Brooks said.

Smith rolled his eyes. "Come on. Just for a few days."

Brooks gave a wary glance. "You know how much can happen in a few days."

"Babe. What's the point of having employees if you're gonna insist on doing half the work?"

---

* Metaphorically, this time.

Brooks shifted a little. "Yeah. But who's going to watch Maria?"

Smith chuckled. "Um, my parents?"

"They won't mind?" Brooks asked.

"They didn't move to New Jersey for their health, babe. Old people live for that shit."

Brooks deliberated for a moment. "Okay."

"Okay?"

"Okay," Brooks said.

Smith kissed him on the forehead, then hopped off the bed. "I'll go call them."

Brooks faked a smile. When Smith was safely out of the room and Brooks could hear his husband's expletive-free phone voice, he flopped backwards onto his pillow and thought hard.

*When did they move to New Jersey?* he wondered.

It seemed to him that a couple in their eighties would be reluctant to abandon their closest relatives and move across the country, and that if they did they would need a lot of assistance. They'd also need help settling in—help that Brooks and Smith would have gladly given them. But he couldn't remember ever having done so. He also couldn't remember when exactly they moved. When he really focused on it, he couldn't even remember when Smith and his parents had reconciled. He didn't think he was crazy, but that's probably what crazy people thought.

He shook his head. *Maybe Eddie's right. Maybe I do need a vacation. It's not like the world can just change overnight.*

# 17 / OVERNIGHT

Patience knelt, pocketknife in hand. Her gown had become an inconvenience, so she slashed at it, then pulled the dress apart until her left leg was visible to the thigh. That afforded her some freedom of movement. With it, she leaped to the right, dodging a three-foot-long mutated sewer rat.*

The creature ran into a wall, but swiftly recovered. It made a quick circle to regain its bearings, then leaped at her again with a fearsome hiss. Patience dodged again, and held her knife out in front of her. The next time it pounced, she'd be ready.

Susie Darkstick was busy fending off two rats of her own, but her eyes remained focused on Patience. The young woman had a natural talent for monster slaying, and Susie smiled. Then she bashed a rat's head in with a hammer.

Patience breathed out, steeling herself. This was it.

The rat hissed and bared its yellow fangs. Even from a few feet away, Patience could see the strands of saliva in its mouth and smell the death on its breath. Claws extended, the creature flew toward her. Patience thrust the knife forward, stabbing it in the chest. A direct hit to the heart. The rat screeched and twitched in a growing puddle of its blood. Then it was still.

Patience wiped the blood off her blade with the fabric she'd torn from her dress. She tucked the knife back into her satchel, grabbed the flashlight she'd set down, and turned to Susie (Ms. Darkstick, as she called her).

"Where to now?" Patience asked. She attempted to growl the question, but her voice was unable to reach the lows that Susie's could.

---

* The fact that it was three feet long had nothing to do with the mutation.

"We keep searching." Susie stowed her hammer in her bag. "We've looked everywhere above ground. Now this."

Two hours beneath New York City and the sewer tunnels had led them nowhere. There were a few overgrown rats, obviously, but little else.

Their partnership was inevitable. As was tradition for a Puritan, Patience had abandoned her family for Kayden's. She'd also reached executive level at the Darkstick Agency in record time. Not due to any talents, per se, but due to her willingness to go along with just about anything. In this case, the 'anything' was a genie hunt. Susie's genie, which had served her reasonably well despite not finding Dev's killer, had disappeared, and she was grasping at sewage-filled straws to find it. Damp shoes and the ghastly smell weren't going to deter either detective, but the younger one had a suggestion.

Patience frowned. "I believe we should seek help in this endeavor."

"Not. Yet." Susie hissed.

"Our search has persisted for months," Patience said. "And though the Darkstick Agency's staff are quite talented, we've found nothing regarding a genie."

The Darkstick Agency's staff was not talented. It consisted of people like Susie—obsessed with proving themselves over actually accomplishing anything. One partner, Ivan Sokolov, summoned an ice demon just so he could defeat it and post the video on YouTube. Instead he died, but the video did go viral.

"We'll find something," Susie said. "With no outside help."

"If you insist..."

Susie pointed to a split in the tunnel and tossed Patience a walkie-talkie. "You go left. I'll go right."

"Of course," Patience said. Flashlight in one hand and walkie-talkie in the other, she hurried left.

Susie wasn't quite as eager. She tapped the tape recorder at her side as she strolled down the path to the right. Her voice deepened for narration. "My partner and I split up, and I have full confidence we'll find what we're after. On a personal note, she's beginning to grow on me. I no longer worry that my son married a creature of the night. Patience is one of us, and together we will find that genie."

# 18 / LUNCH AT TIFFANYS

When they were DINKs,* Brooks and Smith traveled the world. When they were DITDKs,° they did so less often so that they could budget for Patience's serge and thread allowance. Now that thirty percent of their budget went to diapers and a 529 plan, they had less to work with. Their vacation, as a result, took them thirty-seven miles from home.

Tarrytown, New York was no exotic getaway, but it had an inn, which was enough. There had been a brief tizzy when Brooks realized the man checking them into the hotel was also named Edward Smith, but his Smith assured him that, yes, his name really was that generic and, yes, that was to be expected from his biological parents. He further explained that he was lucky those "piece of shit assholes" didn't name him "Dusty, Earl, or Roscoe." That rant was good enough to squelch Brooks's anxiety.

Following a messy romp for which they tipped housekeeping exceptionally well, Brooks and Smith went to lunch. The sign outside Tiffany's clarified that it bore no relationship to any more famous Tiffany's, and that they did not serve breakfast. It was established in 1989 by Tiffany Gretzky, who also bore no relationship to any more famous Gretzkys. The diner had all the shitty hallmarks of a diner: chrome barstools with red leather seats, equally red booths with beige padding poking through tears, a menu with so much variety that nothing on it could exceed adequacy, an old man reading a newspaper like that's a normal thing to do, yokels complaining about paying taxes, and so on.

Tarrytown got tourists when it was close to Halloween and

---

* Dual-income, no kids
° Dual-income, time-displaced kids

Sleepy Hollow was a kitschy place to visit. But in January, Brooks and Smith were the only ones there. The tax-hating citizens gave them the stink eye for violating the sanctity of their diner, and for taking the prime window seat with a view of the Hudson River.

Brooks pulled out a brochure he'd taken from an unmanned tourist info booth. "It says to try the..." He blinked with judgment. "Spaghetti pie."

"What the fuck is a spaghetti pie?" Smith asked.

"Let's see..." Brooks ran a finger down the placemat/menu. "Three pounds of spaghetti and meatballs, baked inside a homemade lattice top pie crust. Served with your choice of mashed potatoes or macaroni and cheese." He frowned. "That's disgusting."

Smith shrugged. "I'll try it."

The waiter—a lanky teenager in horn-rimmed glasses—returned with two glasses of water straight from Tarrytown's municipal water supply. He pulled out his pen and pad and prepared to take their order. "You two know what you want?"

Brooks eyed the waiter's nametag: Eddie. "If you don't mind, Eddie, what's your last name?"

"Smith," the waiter said. "Why?"

"No reason," Brooks said, shooting a pointed glance at his Smith.

"I'll try the spaghetti pie," Smith said to his namemate.

The waiter scribbled. "For your side, do you want mashed potatoes or mac and cheese?"

"Surprise me," said Smith.

The waiter turned to Brooks, his pen ready. "And for you?"

"I'll... share that," Brooks said.

"There's a five dollar plate sharing fee."

"That's fine. Whatever," Brooks said. When the waiter left, he leaned over the booth and whisper-shouted. "Edward

Smith? That's the third one in Tarrytown. This isn't normal."

"You know how many people I've met with my name?" Smith asked.

"With this frequency? Come on. It's another *thing*." Brook sat up straight and ran a hand from his forehead back through his hair.

"I told you. There are *thousands* of me," Smith said, shaking his head. "You really want the world to be broken, don't you?"

"No. I don't. But it is." Brooks drummed the table with his fingers.

"It's not broken. A little shitty? Always. But not broken."

It was, and Brooks knew it. In the three days between *Gilligan's Butte* and their quick trip to Tarrytown, he'd grown increasingly paranoid. The slight something-is-wrong feeling had given way to an oh-God-we're-all-doomed feeling, and he couldn't get Smith to believe him. He hesitated to bring up the biggest lingering question in his mind, but decided he had to. "Why do we have Maria? Why did you agree to adopt? How the hell did the paperwork go through so quickly?"

"I love her. *You* love her," Smith said.

Brooks stared into his eyes. "Of course I do. That's not what I asked."

"I got shot in the face and did the 'life flashing before my eyes' thing. You know that." Smith squinted. "Are you missing chunks of time or what?"

Brooks ignored the question and pushed. "But *why* did you agree? You've said yourself worse things have happened. And why don't you have a scar on your face? You were shot in the face!"

"Coincidence?" Smith offered. "What about the pole in the skull guy?"

"Phineas Gage? He had a scar. He also went crazy!"

A few diners' stink eyes became stinkier at Brooks's raised

voice.

"Maybe I went my version of crazy," Smith offered.

Brooks tried to make fists to steady himself, but his fingers fluttered. "We've both died before. Patience died before. It's not that weird. I mean... yes it's weird, but that's the world we live in. It's not enough to have freaked you out. It's just not." His voice cracked. "Something isn't right."

As if on cue, a commercial blared from the diner's television. A recognizable saxophone jingle, followed by a recognizable sleazy announcer. "Have you or a loved one died and resurrected as a cyborg? If so, we want to hear from you. Call 888-555-DONNA and you could be featured in an upcoming episode."

Brooks's face went white. "That's *oddly specific*, don't you think?"

Smith frowned. "A little. Maybe someone we know talked to someone who works on the show."

"Come on," Brooks said.

"It's a reasonable explanation. Or it had nothing to do with us. Who knows how many people the Reticent turned into cyborgs?"

He had a point, which annoyed Brooks. "Yeah."

"You haven't been going to therapy," Smith noted.

"I haven't needed to," Brooks said.

"You haven't been practicing the Q.U.E.E.R. Method either."*

"I haven't needed to," Brooks repeated.

Smith took a sip of water. "You sure?"

Brooks leaned back in the booth, pointed his face to the ceiling, and ran his hands through his hair again. When he returned to Smith's eye level, his voice was deliberate. "I'm

---

* The Q.U.E.E.R. Method was a five-step meditation technique developed by Doctor Queer, Earth's Divine Dimensionmaster and former roommate of Brooks's. It consisted of quiet reflection followed by rubbing one out.

serious. It's not anxiety. It's not PTSD. I'm not crazy. Something is wrong."

"Okay," Smith said with a halfhearted shrug.

"You don't believe me," Brooks said.

"I don't feel the same way," Smith said. "Doesn't mean I don't believe you."

"That's exactly what it means," Brooks said.

"No. I believe something is wrong *for you*. Burroughs can run a diagnostic when we get back, but in the meantime there's nothing you can do about it. So—"

"Enjoy myself," Brooks said. "Yeah. I'm tryi—"

TINK PLINK TINK. Outside, three bees charged into the window and dropped to the ground.

Brooks gestured at the window. "—That's another thing!"

Smith rolled his eyes. "What?"

"Have there always been so many roving swarms of bees?"

Smith answered with confidence. "Yeah, babe. There have."

"Even in the winter?" Brooks asked.

Smith cocked his head. "Uhh... yeah."

Brooks slumped again. "If I'm going crazy, you have to help me."

Smith put a hand on his arm. "I will. I'm sure it's just a bug or something."

"Okay." Brooks reoriented himself and gazed out the window. TINK PLINK TINK. He tried to ignore it, but everything in his mind wanted to reject this reality. He shut his eyes and tried to remember the first time he saw a swarm of bees. Nothing.

After a minute or so, the waiter returned with a steaming pie. He tossed a potholder onto the table and set it down, along with a spatula for serving, then hurried back to the kitchen. Strands of spaghetti in red sauce poked out from the top of the crust, their tips burnt.

"It looks like it's full of maggots," Brooks said.

Smith shrugged. "It's spaghetti."

The waiter returned, bearing a huge, equally hot bowl of macaroni and cheese that came from a box. "Is there anything else I can get you?"

"Nope," Smith said.

"Enjoy!"

Brooks blinked. "Pasta with a side of pasta..."

"Pasta *pie* with a side of pasta," Smith corrected. "Get it right."

"There's nothing right about it," Brooks said.

Smith grabbed the spatula and carved out a loosely held-together clump of spaghetti pie. It landed on his plate with the sound of a wet mop hitting linoleum. Brooks scowled and served himself a slice. His eyes studied it. Something was off, so he activated a setting and zoomed in. He'd been right before: the spaghetti sauce contained dead maggots, dead flies, and at least one dead cockroach.

Brooks looked up and gave a horrified gasp as Smith took a bite. "*Oh my God.* The pie is full of dead bugs."

Smith swallowed, then eyed Brooks with concern. "Yeah. What do you think spaghetti *is*?"

# 19 / TO THE CONNERS GO THE SPOILS

As celebrating people do, Solange Conner popped a bottle of fine champagne. *The Guinness Book of World Records* had just registered the Conner Building as the world's tallest LEED-certified green building. It sat where the Empire State Building—tragically lost in a sinkhole—once had. There was no reason Rhett needed to buy the site, other than the fact that he could. Another award was another award, and it amused him to see newspapers running pictures of a building that had been designed as a tall, rounded shaft with a bulbous tip. He was an artist, he said, and it was an important statement.

Wealth wasn't Rhett's end goal, but it sure was nice. People had started treating him better once he un-balded his head and made his face and body gorgeous, and the money added to the preferential treatment. Hundreds of New York's richest had gathered for the type of celebration where tuxedoed servers in white gloves served apéritifs. The tablecloths alone cost more than the New York median household income, and Rhett and Solange sat behind one at a table, alone.

"I don't like these tablecloths," Rhett said. "They look cheap."

"You could change them," Solange said.

"No," Rhett cautioned. "I don't want these rich assholes to know about the djinn until it's too late. Plus, if I changed them I wouldn't have anything to complain to the decorator about."

Solange faked a smile as she poured two glasses of vegan champagne to soften his mood. "Never mind that. Congratulations."

"Yeah," Rhett mumbled, taking a glass.

She extended an arm and clinked her glass to his.

"To us," Solange said.

It should have been a sweet, innocent toast. Instead, Rhett set his glass down and scowled.

"*Us?*" He leaned his head on his fist and stared at her.

Solange frowned. She was beginning to realize that her husband's constant frustration was not the result of stress, but of being a douchebag. They had everything now: the djinn, money, fame, influence, good looks, and all the classy parties they could handle. Still Rhett was a dick.

Rhett continued staring at her. "What exactly did *you* do that you deserve a toast?"

Solange offered a weak reply. "I did the research..."

"Oh. Some *research*. That's a lot. Wow. See, I was under the impression that *I* found the djinn and that *I* built all of this for us." He made a sweeping gesture at the room.

Solange lowered her head. "Sorry."

"You're not, or you would have just toasted *me*," Rhett said. "Not *us*."

Solange's eyes shifted. "What?"

Rhett drew out the words as he repeated himself. "Why do you feel like you need to take credit?"

"I don't. It, uh... was a joke."

"You sure?" Rhett asked. "It wasn't funny."

Solange shrank into her seat. "I told you I'm sorry."

"Then why did you say it?" Rhett asked.

"I—"

He leaned toward her with a menacing scowl. "You know what?"

Solange leaned back. "What?"

"I'm done with you," Rhett said.

Solange got up and set her glass down. There was no reason to get a djinn involved. "I'll go."

"Yeah. You will." Rhett smirked.

Solange had a feeling she—like the rich assholes—wasn't

going to make it out of that room.

# 20 / SPAGHETTI != MAGGOTS

For Brooks's dignity, he covered himself with a blanket. That way, if someone were to burst into the room they wouldn't see his USB port. He lay on a cot, cord extended to Burroughs's laptop. ADHOC's research laboratory was modest, but a big improvement over the nonexistent research lab they had a few months earlier.

Brooks tried to fill the silence with awkward small talk. "So in Tarrytown..."

"Working," Burroughs said. She didn't bother to look up from the screen. No one wanted to hear about Tarrytown.

Brooks sighed. His eyes darted around the room, taking in motivational poster after motivational poster. They'd seemed like a good idea when he approved them, but he now realized that having Teamwork, Perseverance, Motivation, Potential, Gratitude, and Ambition was just too much.

Burroughs announced the results of her scan. "No viruses or evil programming."

Brooks shook his head. "I'm losing my mind then. I'm crazy. This is it."

"Relax," Burroughs said, never removing her eyes from the screen. "It would help if you gave me more to work with than 'things seem off.'"

"I don't have a better way of describing it," he said. "I just think... spaghetti is wrong, and I can't remember details."

"Details? Like what?"

"Like, when did Eddie's parents move to New Jersey from Indiana? I know they did, but if I focus on it, I can't figure out when."

"It was in November," Burroughs said. She remembered it clearly because watching Maria that day was one of the six things Smith owed her for.

Brooks shook his head. "Or... like... how long did it take Eddie to recover from being shot in the face? I don't remember ever going to the hospital, which is stupid. I definitely would have been there."

Burroughs squinted in consideration. "You *were* there. Are you sure you don't want him here now?"

Brooks glanced under the blanket. "I'm sure I don't want *anyone* here."

"I'm sure he's seen your port by now," Burroughs said.

"We wouldn't be married if he didn't stare at my port a few times a week," Brooks said. "Still. The less anyone sees me as a machine, the better."

"I don't think he sees you as a machine, but okay..." Burroughs hit a few keys and mumbled. Out of nowhere, her voice perked up in interest. "Oh!"

"What?" Brooks asked.

"Whoops," Burroughs said, eyes darting around the screen.

Brooks shot forward and tried to comprehend the screen. He couldn't. "*Whoops?*"

"I know what the problem is." Burroughs gritted her teeth. "Your latest patch errored out, and your system got restored to an old backup."

"How old?" Brooks asked.

"Three months," Burroughs said. "It should have gone to the one we did last week. Geez. No wonder you've been confused. It backed up to before some *major* life changes."

Brooks shook his head. "But I *remember* the last three months. Mostly. Eddie and I would have noticed something was wrong if I didn't recognize my own daughter."

Burroughs squinted at the screen. "This is weird."

"What's weird?"

"Your event log—"

"Dumb it down," Brooks said. He left college a few credits shy of a bachelor's degree in chemistry, and that was twelve years ago.

She hovered her finger in front of the screen, taking in the information. "The three month backup and last week's don't look anything alike."

"What do you mean?"

"Your backups are cumulative. Basically, we just add new memories each time. You have a backup, then two weeks later, we add the last two weeks' worth of information to the old backup."

"Okay..."

"So information doesn't get replaced or altered."

"Okay..."

"Except I made a checksum and things *have* changed."

Brooks's face lost all expression. "So I *do* have evil programming again?"

"No. But someone or something has tampered with your memories," Burroughs said. "It'll take a while, but I can compare the files and see what's changed. This is... this could be bad."

"Bad how?" Brooks wondered. "I'm not crazy, so you'll just fix it and we're good."

Her face and voice disagreed. "Arturo..."

"What?" Brooks asked.

"It might be better if you *were* crazy. Someone tampered with your brain. Someone *has the ability* to tamper with your brain."

"How can someone do that?" Brooks asked. "Why would someone do that?"

Burroughs answered the two questions with two responses. "I don't know, and I don't know. Maybe you did it to yourself."

"Excuse me?"

"Maybe something happened and you couldn't deal with it, so you altered your own memories," she suggested.

"So maybe I *am* crazy?"

"You're really focused on the crazy thing, and not the implications..." Burroughs trailed off and read something on her screen. "Judging from the file sizes alone, there are going to be some huge differences."

"Huge how?"

"I don't know. *Huge.* Are you sure you're going to be able to deal with that?"

"I guess we'll see when we find out what happened. But for now I'm not crazy." He said it like it was a victory.

Burroughs rolled her eyes. "You might be when I'm done."

Several hours' worth of technobabble and abandoned small talk later, Burroughs had a breakthrough. Brooks looked up from a texted image of a diaper explosion labeled 'why' in time to catch her look of shock.

"It's not your memories that have been altered," she said.

"What do you mean?" Brooks asked. "Your computer's broken?"

Burroughs shook her head and spoke softly. "It's reality. Your memories are consistent from your birth to three months ago. Well, as consistent as human memories are anyway. Then they change. So I tried uploading my own consciousness using AfterAfterlife, and it errored out."

Brooks tilted his head. "Isn't that illegal?"

"It is, but the point is, you're not broken. Reality is."

"Broken how?"

"I don't know."

Brooks repeated himself, as if that would change her answer. "*Broken how?*"

"I. Don't. Know. I can't access my old memories and I'm not invading yours."

"Well, how do we find out what changed?" Brooks asked.

She hesitated. "I can give you both." Burroughs thought

out loud. "If your brain could hold seventy-some afterlife scenarios and Eddie's mind at the same time, I'm sure it can hold two sets of your own memories. Instead of restoring the old backup, I could put a partition in there and you'd have... both."

"Okay. So do that."

"You're way too willing to have me mess around in your head," Burroughs said. "I'm not qualified to say it won't make you bonkers."

"Well, we have to know, right?"

"Yeah, but..."

"Then do it."

Burroughs hesitated. "Are you sure you don't want me to call Eddie first?"

"I'm sure," Brooks said. "Do it."

"I'd just like to remind you that you're always on Eddie's ass for keeping things from you, and this is a huge thing to keep from him."

Brooks was too intent on getting answers to mind his hypocrisy. "Noted. Now do it."

# 21 / RACE TO THE BOTTOM

Patience approached the retina scanner like she approached most things: with discomfort. She'd gotten braver, sure, but she still made it a rule to avoid eye contact, even with machines. The scanner beeped in approval, and the door unlocked with a KRSHT. She shuffled inside and made her way down a pink corridor lined with black raven wall-clings and illuminated by black chandeliers. This was the Darkstick Agency, and all décor met Susie's personal approval.

From speakers above came the emo music that was pumped into the office 24/7.

*Life is never faaaaaiiirrrrr*
*Feel it in the aaaaaairrrrr*

Kayden leaned against a wall, as usual. He never seemed to be working. "Hey."

Patience stopped to greet him with a "hello."

He scrunched his nose. "Did you get attacked by a trash monster?"

Patience shook her head. "I was asked to investigate the garbage dump." She exhaled a tiny snort to illustrate her dismay.

"Ugh." Kayden flipped his hair back off his face. "She's still got you working on that?"

"Yes. It's most vexing," said Patience.

"I wish there was a way to make her stop obsessing," Kayden said. "It's not like there isn't other stuff she can do to occupy her time."

There was plenty of 'other stuff' to do. It seemed everyone in New York had been accosted by some creature or another, and dozens of second-rate paranormal detective agencies had sprung up to deal with them. But none of them had the pull or pizzazz of the Darkstick Agency.

"I'll speak with her again," Patience said, resuming her shuffle.

Kayden grabbed her arm. "When you're done, maybe we can beat her home and, you know."

Patience's cheeks flushed. "Perhaps."

In 2017, it was rare for a couple not to consummate their relationship before marriage, let alone after. But Patience had managed a month's worth of excuses. She couldn't remember why she'd agreed to marry so quickly, and she certainly didn't want to rush into even more serious matters—especially before she figured out her stance on birth control. She fretted down the hallway.

Two burly security officers guarded Susie's office, but they let Patience through.

Susie was pumping, and the sight of her breasts affixed to whirring suction cups gave Patience further motivation to avoid her husband. The Puritan fanned herself a little.

Susie shouted over the noise. "Did you find it?"

"No," Patience said. She took a seat on the other side of the desk. "Ms. Darkstick—"

"You're family. It's just Susie."

Patience lowered her head. "In any case, I don't believe we're meant to find a genie."

"I had it before," Susie said. "It's *mine*."

"Have you considered that perhaps it never existed?" Patience asked. She and Kayden had talked this over a number of times, and he couldn't remember anything that indicated his mom had ever had a genie.

Susie didn't take kindly to the suggestion. "What? You think I just *made it up* so I could cope with Dev's death?"

Never one to recognize sarcasm, Patience nodded. "Precisely."

"It wasn't a coping mechanism," Susie said. "It was in my

necklace. It's blue, sort of like a cloud."

"As in the film *Aladdin*?" Patience asked.

"Yes. Exactly. Maybe that's the problem. I haven't described it well enough so you don't know exactly what you're looking for."

"Or perhaps you imagined it to look like a famous fictional character?"

Susie's pump shut off, and she tapped her tape recorder. "I don't like where this is going," she narrated. "Patience is beginning to question my methods and, I believe, my very sanity."

Patience frowned. "Perhaps—"

"Perhaps," Susie narrated, "I made a mistake making her a partner so soon. Perhaps her loyalties still lie with her fathers. Perhaps she and my son are plotting to overthrow me and steal my company. So many potential conspiracies. I'll need to dig deeper. Find out what's going on." She stopped recording.

Patience knew her next thought would arouse Susie's suspicion, but she offered it anyway. "Perhaps we should enlist the help of additional detective agencies. If others knew we were seeking a genie, they could inform us about anomalies."

"Other agencies like *ADHOC*?" Susie asked. "Out of the question."

"Not necessarily. What about Vamp's Ire? Investigations 'R' Us? Conner Inquiries?"

Susie pointed at Patience. "No. Anyone who finds out we're looking for a genie will try to steal it for themselves. If they haven't already." She realized that was an important thought, and tapped the record button again. "Patience brings up a good point. Another agency may have already found the genie. If they did, surely they'd be extremely successful. Too successful." The narration ended with the tap of a button, but Susie continued talking to herself. "Rhett Conner."

"Pardon?" Patience asked.

"He has a hand in every industry. Pharmaceuticals, space exploration, online banking, farming... And his detective business is growing at an alarming rate."

Patience sighed, in her mind. "I believe his business is growing on account of advertising. He has far more money with which to purchase billboards, television spots..."

"Right. Or he found my genie." Susie put a hand to her chin. "From now on, we're doubling the advertising budget. And I'm going to pay Rhett Conner a visit."

"As you wish," Patience said, lowering her head. She had a different idea—one she could take into her own hands.

On her way out, she passed Kayden once more.

"Heading home?" He never smiled, but his voice perked up slightly at the notion of losing his virginity.

"Oh. Hmm. I'm afraid I'm needed at another investigation," Patience said. "We'll have to engage in marital relations another time."

"That's cool, I guess. I'll go out and catch some butterflies or something."

Patience scurried off.

# 22 / WHAT A WONDERFUL WORLD

Smith bided his time between changings watching Old TV with a sleeping Widget at his side. When Brooks returned, Smith didn't realize it at first, as his partner had opened the door as softly as possible and skulked through the doorway. Abandoning his normal ritual of carefully removing his coat and dirty shoes, Brooks took a few steps toward the couch and stopped. In a daze, he stared at Smith, a mixture of suspicious and heartbroken.

Widget perked up and yapped, and Brooks gave him a pathetic rub. The dog scoffed and curled back into a ball.

Smith finally noticed his husband's presence, as well as his mood. "You okay? Get your memories fixed?"

Brooks shook his head.

Smith stood and moved in close to him. "What happened?"

"I wasn't imagining it," Brooks said, sullen. "You should be dead."

"Wow. Thanks."

Brooks buried his head in Smith's shoulder for a moment to compose himself. It didn't work very well, and he shook a little and sniffed as he pulled his head away to speak. "I'm not kidding. Reality was changed three months ago."

"What are you talking about?" Smith asked.

"It's not my brain," Brooks said. "It's not me. I haven't changed. The world has."

"How do you know that? And how do you know it was three months—"

"My backup file was completely different one week to the next. Everything changed. *Everything.*"

"So someone messed with your files."

"No," Brooks said. "We went over that. It's Burroughs

too. It's everyone. Reality changed. *Everything changed.*"

"Everything?" Smith wondered. He took Brooks's arm and guided him toward the couch. "Come on. Sit down."

Brooks complied and stared at nothing. "We were working in a total shithole. It was just us."

"Yeah. We only had the basement office. I know," Smith said.

"Do you remember us taking the time to earn more money and establish a real firm? We didn't. One week it's just us, the next we have a bunch of employees and business is booming."

"That's ridiculous. I remember working twelve-hour days for months."

"No you don't," Brooks said. "It never happened."

Smith squinted. "So everyone has false memories except you. Is that it?"

"No," Brooks said. "I have false memories too... now. I remember everything the way it really was, *and* everything the way you think it was. It's... not great." The burden showed on his face.

"How the hell did that happen?" Smith asked.

"Erin offered and I accepted."

Smith was somewhat annoyed by that, but he let it go for Brooks's sake. "So I was dead. What else changed?"

"I can't—"

Smith put his hands on Brooks's shoulders. "What else changed?"

Brooks started small. "One day, Pop Tart & the Activation Energy are trash. The next they're world famous. Patience became a vampire hunter literally overnight. She got married overnight. We wouldn't have let her get married at eighteen. That's ridiculous."

The TV announcer caught his attention. "Up next is *Gilligan's Butte.*"

Brooks pointed at the TV. "It was an island, not a butte!"

His shout bothered Maria, and she began fussing.

"I've got it." Smith picked her up out of her bassinet.

Brooks's face could never go as white as Smith's, but it tried.

"What's wrong?" Smith asked.

"Maria just... appeared. We didn't go through the adoption process." Brooks started to panic, and rattled off a list of changes. "The Empire State Building. There was never a sinkhole. You were fatter and your parents still lived in Indiana. You didn't talk to them. Burroughs used to be a brunette. Now she's blonde. Roving packs of bees aren't normal. Spaghetti isn't supposed to have bugs in it."

"Well, shit," Smith said. It was a little understated for someone who'd just found out reality had been radically altered. Still holding Maria, he parked next to Brooks. "What do you want to do?"

Brooks freaked. "This is bad. This is so bad."

"If reality did a three-sixty, I'd say so. Yeah."

In less dire times, Brooks would have corrected that to one-eighty, since three hundred and sixty degrees is a full circle. Instead, Brooks just shook his head at his mathematically challenged husband and their daughter. "This reality is good."

Smith nodded. "It's not bad."

"We're successful. Lemon is successful. Patience is successful at whatever the hell they do over there. Who knows what kind of freak would have adopted Maria. Maybe she didn't exist at all. Eddie—" Brooks leaned on Smith's shoulder again. "*Your life* is so much better. Remember the woo-woo doctor?"

"Like I could forget that hot mess," Smith said. "It's not every day you have your husband's memories shoved into your head." He paused in contemplation, as this was actually the second time that had happened to them.

In less dire times, Brooks would have made a sarcastic

remark about that very fact. Instead, he pressed on. "I remember both sets of yours. Before reality changed and after. Believe me when I say... you're much better off. We're *all* so much better off." He reached a finger toward Maria, who grabbed it with her hand and gave a little SQUEE.

Smith looked down at Maria, then at Brooks. "Okay. All we know right now is that something paranormal happened. So what's our job?"

"To figure it out," Brooks sighed.

"We don't need to ruin our lives just yet," Smith said. "We just need to know what happened."

"But—"

"Stay with me, here. We have to figure this out. Something changing reality has a good chance of being a threat."

"Yeah. I know. But—"

Smith spoke deliberately. "We'll worry about the details when we get there."

"I'm worried about the details *now*."

"Exactly," Smith said. "If I was some monster getting ready to destroy everything, I'd want you preoccupied. You have freaky cyborg strength and shit."

Brooks didn't need to be reminded of that. "Yeah..."

"We need to figure it out," Smith said.

"Okay," Brooks said.

Smith thought for a second. "What's the last correct memory you have? Where does everything divert?"

Brooks analyzed the two sets of memories. "It was that stupid woo-woo doctor."

"Then I'll call my parents to watch Maria and we'll go back to the woo-woo doctor."

# 23 / WOO

The day was too perfect—the day equivalent of a flawlessly frosted Pinterest cupcake, resting atop a doily on a tiny cake stand. Sunshine illuminated everything, no one needed a coat, and on every corner groups of people chitchatted or helped the elderly cross the street. In a three-block walk, Brooks and Smith hadn't heard a single car horn. So it stood to reason that something gruesome was going on in the background. Seemingly out of nowhere, R.E.M.'s "Shiny Happy People" began to play at department store volume.

Smith glanced around, trying to locate the source. "Weird."

"What's weird is I was just thinking about that song," Brooks said.

"You were thinking about early-nineties jangle pop?"

Brooks gestured to his left, where a traffic cop agreed to forgive a ticket. He gestured to his right, where a pair of tracksuit-wearing Russian thugs released a dove.

"It looks like a cheesy movie montage," Brooks said.

"Yeah, but I was thinking more 'Raindrops Keep Falling on My Head.'"

"Shiny Happy People" faded out, and "Raindrops Keep Falling on my Head" began to play.

"Okay." Smith glanced up at the apartment windows above him. "You may be right about something being wrong."

"*I know I am.* Glad you're finally on board, though." Something aside from the music felt off, and Brooks turned to look behind them. Nothing.

"You okay?" Smith asked.

Brooks narrowed his eyes. "Yeah..."

They continued on their way, but the music followed them. Smith didn't get it. "So somebody hacked your brain and now they're playing crappy music to taunt us? What the hell is going on here?"

"I don't know," Brooks said. "Maybe it's all part of a distraction."

"Could be. We won't notice someone opening a portal to hell if we're busy investigating the source of Michael Stipe and Burt Bacharach."

"Right. But that assumes whoever's doing something thinks we're a big threat. In that case, you'd think they'd be going after Darkstick or Investigation Tree. We're small fish."

"Again, you're a cyborg," Smith said. "We may not have many clients going for us, but that's gotta be worth something."

"Yeah. I guess we just have to hope we find *something* at the woo-woo doctor."

Still searching for the source of the music, Brooks glanced over his shoulder again, and a small figure darted behind a dumpster.

Brooks continued walking. "Someone's following us."

"Is that you being paranoid, or are—"

Brooks stopped, turned, and stepped toward the dumpster.

"—you sure?"

Armed with cyborg strength, Brooks rounded the corner of the dumpster, ready to fight. Smith followed, ready to observe a fight. There was a slight peep.

Brooks relaxed at the sight of a familiar face. "What are you doing here?"

"Following you, sirs," Patience said.

Brooks scrunched his nose. "Were you hiding in the dumpster?"

"No. The smell is from a case. I was investi—"

Smith choked back a laugh. "You're working cases now?"

"Of course," Patience said. "Toil is virtue."

"Why were you following us?" Brooks asked.

She frowned. "It's about Ms. Darkstick."

Smith stepped to the side and smacked his forehead. "We don't care."

Brooks nudged him. "Eddie."

"What? We don't."

Brooks nudged him again, then spoke to Patience. "What is it?"

"*We don't care,*" Smith repeated.

With Brooks nodding at her, Patience continued. "She's trying to find her missing genie. Have either of you seen one?"

This time, Smith let himself break into laughter. "Her *genie?*" While plenty of supernatural creatures existed, genies were basically Santa Claus—believed in only by children and kind of creepy if you really thought about the implications.

Brooks turned pale. Something in that word got his neurons firing.

"Oh, Christ," Smith said. He crossed his arms.

Patience squirmed a little at the blasphemy.

Smith stared at Brooks. "Genies aren't ridiculous now?"

"It's fuzzy, but... I feel like someone else was looking for a genie," Brooks said.

Patience perked up, recalling her conversation with Susie, and one name in particular: *Rhett Conner.* Her fathers had mentioned his name in the past, and Patience determined that it meant something.

"When was someone looking for a genie?" Smith asked.

Brooks had no confidence in his mind. "I don't know. Other things are so clear but this... maybe it didn't happen..."

"Gonna need better than that," Smith said.

Brooks snapped back. "Well I'm sorry if I get confused having *four sets of memories.*"

Smith raised his hands in defense. "Okay. Fair."

"I want to say we were both there, but..." Brooks trailed

off, unable to finish the thought.

"Have you seen one then?" Patience asked.

"Uh, no," Brooks said.

"Hmm. Well, I suppose I'll go meet Ms. Darkstick at the *Conner Building*." Patience had seen enough television that she knew to wink for emphasis. Unfortunately, some dysfunction left her unable to close only one eye at a time. She ended up looking like she had dust in her eyes.

"What's Susie doing at the Conner Building?" Smith asked.

Patience shook her head. "That's proprietary information."

"Oh, for—"

Brooks cut in. "Someone or something is altering reality. If you know anything about it, please tell us. Whatever contract you signed isn't as big as what's happening."

"It's unrelated to your case," Patience said. "I believe she's seeking advertising tips. Perhaps you would do well to try the same?"

Patience had lied. It wasn't a half-truth. It wasn't a quarter-truth. It wasn't even an eighth-truth. She knew Susie suspected Rhett might have a genie, but family was family and an NDA was an NDA. The best she could hope to do was leave Brooks and Smith intrigued enough to visit the Conner Building.

Smith's brow wrinkled in thought. "Did you just insult us for not having enough clients?"

Patience sighed. He hadn't gotten the hint. "I'm simply saying it may be beneficial to seek *Mr. Conner's* advice." She blinked hard.

"Do you need some Visine?" Brooks asked.

Patience shook her head. "No. I do recommend convening with Mr. Conner, though."

"Fuck that guy," Smith said.

"Yeah. He's the worst," Brooks said.

"I'll be there," Patience said. "If that would change your

minds."

"It doesn't," Smith said.

Patience deflated. "Very well. I must be on my way."

"Take care of yourself," Brooks said. "Seriously."

"I will." Patience sighed again and fretted into the distance.

"She seem weird to you?" Smith asked.

"Always. Not much more than usual, though."

There were three people on the planet—at best—capable of recognizing a Gin Blossoms song other than "Hey Jealousy." Brooks was one of them, and as they continued down the road such a song began to play.

"Goddamn it," Smith said. "Stop thinking about nineties jangle pop."

Brooks glared, and the music got louder.

# 24 / HOW THE HELL DO YOU DEFEAT A GENIE?

Pleasant Humans was nothing like Brooks or Smith remembered. Leon still ran the register, but the whole place had lost its sense of woo-woo. Shards of rattan stuck out from what little wicker furniture remained. Half-cleared shelves contained expired products that bore bright orange CLEARANCE stickers.* There was no music, just the garbled noise of whatever video Leon was watching on his phone. In the back of the shop, Vinegret's office was boarded up, and her list of treatments had been erased. All that remained were chalk smudges.

"What happened here?" Brooks asked.

Unaccustomed to customers, Leon grunted. "What?"

"What happened here? Shouldn't business be booming with all the paranormal activity lately?"

"Would be if Vinegret hadn't left," Leon said.

Smith ran a finger across a dusty shelf. "She just left?"

"Yeah. Weirdest thing. I'm still getting automatic deposits, though." Leon shrugged.

"When did she leave?" Brooks asked.

"Uh." Leon exhaled. "It's been a while. Few months at least."

Brooks and Smith shared a knowing glance.

"Would you say it's been about three months?" Smith asked.

Leon pursed his lips. "Yeah, that sounds about right."

Brooks pulled Smith out of the cashier's earshot. It didn't matter because Leon didn't care what they were talking about

---

* Expiration did not affect their efficacy.

and continued watching his video.

"We were here three months ago," Brooks said. "It's probably not a coincidence my backup is from the same time Vinegret disappeared. The same time you were shot. The same time everything changed. Whatever happened, it started here."

Smith's eyes shifted around as he tried to recall something. "Rhett."

"Rhett Conner? You think Darkstick is onto something?"

"No. She's an idiot." Smith waved a finger in the air as he remembered. "But Rhett was here. Remember?"

Brooks gave him a puzzled look.

Smith's eyes went wide. "No, you don't. You were all fucked up on the woo-woo, but when we left our appointment, Rhett was here. He and Solange were going in for theirs."

"Oh no," Brooks said. He searched his memories—his real memories—but all he could remember was the woo-woo pain. "Are you sure?"

"If I have to trust you that the entire world changed overnight, you have to trust me on this," Smith said. "And you know what Rhett was looking for?"

The fog in Brooks's mind lifted. "A genie..."

"A genie." Smith took a deep breath. "Fuck. How did we forget about the genie? Did he make us forget about the genie?" He stopped asking questions. "He never killed a dragon and stole its treasure. Rhett has a *fucking genie*."

"All of his success... the whole world is different..." Brooks pulled himself out of thought and back into detective mode. "So he found Susie's genie. First thing he did was come here and get rid of the woo-woo therapist?"

"If they got the couples energy sync and it went like ours, it makes sense. He could have erased her from reality..." Smith started.

Brooks finished for him. "And that might have caused the

fog. You can't remember what doesn't exist."

Smith shook his head. "But it's probably broader than that. No one's gonna waste one of three wishes on just a woo-woo therapist. Maybe he disappeared everyone who wronged him. We need to look into his enemies—"

"We're sort of his enemies and we're still here," Brooks noted.

"True. We did *forget about him*, though. That could be genie magic."

"Are we even sure it's three wishes?" Brooks asked.

"We're not sure of anything, but it was in *Aladdin*."

"Oh. Well in that case, I'm getting a tiger for a pet."

Smith rolled his eyes. "Whatever number of wishes, the next thing he does is make himself rich."

"Rich *and* successful *and* admired," Brooks said. "He could have changed the world so he was born wealthy, but no. It had to be a dragon slaying. God. He's such a tool we should have realized something was wrong."

"But we didn't," Smith said. "You think he wished he wouldn't be found out?"

Brooks pulled out some sass. "Probably not, since we're on his trail now."

"True."

Brooks made his way to a broken wicker couch and sat down. It buckled a little. Smith sat next to him, and it buckled a little more.

"What are we going to do?" Brooks asked.

"Defeat a guy with a genie," Smith said with zero confidence.

"*How*? How do you defeat 'phenomenal cosmic power'?"

"By trapping it in a lamp, I guess? You read the books. No one knows anything about them, or if they do we can't translate it."

"Eddie, we're screwed."

"We've thought that before," Smith said.*

"Really, though. We don't know anything, and the only way to find out how it works is to confront him." Brooks tensed as he described their predicament. "If he still has wishes, he can kill us in a second. If we somehow defeat him, it might set everything back to the way it was three months ago. Or it might not. We might be stuck with a reality that he's altered, with whatever ripple effects that has. My God, Donald Trump is President in this world. You think he didn't have something to do with that?"

"I don't know," Smith said. "Do you want to just ignore it and let him get away with it, though?"

Brooks rubbed at his temples for a moment and sighed. "No? I guess. It's too dangerous for someone to have that much power. I know." He spoke to convince himself. "I know we have to try and stop him. I know."

"Well, you're our best hope," Smith said. "Your backup file didn't change, so there's *something* about you that resists genie magic. Maybe you can steal his lamp or whatever."

Brooks answered with trepidation. "Yeah... Eddie."

"What?"

Brooks shut his eyes to keep his composure. When he opened them, he spoke slowly. "I don't want to lose our daughter."

"Neither do I," Smith said. "But it's not about us. If he's out there making people disappear and meddling with the bees, we have to try to stop him."

"Do we?" Brooks asked. He already knew the answer.

Smith stared at him. "You know we do."

"You were dead," Brooks said. "I don't want to lose you either."

---

* As of January 2017, Brooks had thought the words "we're screwed" a total of 481 times. Smith had thought the same words a total of 212 times. If thoughts of "we're fucked" are included, Brooks's grand total was 519, while Smith's was 9,167.

"Since when has death stopped me from being a pain in your ass?" Smith asked. "I'm sure there's a copy of me in the cloud *somewhere*."

That was a fair point, and Brooks nodded, though he didn't fancy doing the superhero thing again to get Smith another clone body.

"How long have we been in this line of work?" Smith asked.

"Over a decade," Brooks said.

"You know how things will go if we don't do something."

Brooks knew exactly how paranormal things tended to go: poorly. He nodded. "So... do we tell everyone what we're doing? I mean, Rhett could just kill us and make Maria an orphan. *Oh God*. She could have her whole family massacred and grow up to be a wreck like me." He leaned back.

Like Brooks, the wicker seat couldn't take any more. It collapsed, sending both men ass-first onto the ground. Leon looked up for half a second before returning to his videos.

# 25 / ACCESS DENIED

Patience had completed all six of the Darkstick Agency's mandatory online training courses, and as a Certified Paranormal Detective - Junior Level, she was well-versed in Building Entry. She circled the Connor Building a few times, touristy map spread out between her hands. Tucked into it was the Darkstick Agency's Investigative Checklist, and Patience's eyes darted from it to the building and back as she shuffled around the block.

There were several problems. First, there were no security cameras. Protocol demanded that Patience locate such devices and disable them, to avoid being captured on film. If she couldn't locate the cameras, she couldn't check the box. If she couldn't check the box, she couldn't proceed. Second, there were no security guards. Every detective at the Darkstick Agency knew there were two types of security guard. There was the overzealous guard with a chip on his shoulder—the type of guard who wouldn't hesitate to pepper spray a ten-year-old. The other type was the lazy guard, who could be found napping or watching Netflix behind his desk. But a brief foray into the Conner Building lobby revealed neither. It revealed nothing at all, and that was the third problem: there was no one at all inside the Conner Building. In Manhattan. In the middle of the day. It was utterly baffling.

All the signs of people were there. The heavy-duty tile flooring that could stand up to traffic. The ambient muzak. The flat screen TVs showing corporate propaganda videos. The backlit sign that read "CONNER" in a tasteful sans-serif font. It should have been teeming. The front desk should have been manned, and the phone should have been ringing. Patience should have been accosted, scanned for weapons, and given a visitor's badge at the security checkpoint. But none of that happened. She looked left, then right, then left again. She scanned the ceiling, the floor, and everything in between (i.e., walls).

Patience decided to break protocol and investigate anyway. Ms. Darkstick wouldn't mind, after all, if Patience were to rescue her from some precarious situation. She looked down at her investigative checklist and frowned. Forging paperwork was a line she wouldn't cross, as she believed signatures entailed a sacred promise. She checked "no" next to "Did you disable the security cameras?" and stepped toward the elevators, only to be pushed backward by some invisible force. Patience stumbled and fell to the floor, puzzled. A "hmm" escaped her mouth.

Patience kept her eyes fixed forward, hoping to catch a glimpse of whatever had shoved her. But again, it was an invisible force, so she didn't see anything. She dusted herself off and prepared for another run at it. Then from nowhere came a jaunty country song, courtesy of Trev Cracklin.

*In the back of a truck, down on my luck...*

Patience jumped back in surprise, as she always did when her phone rang. On its screen, "Incoming Call: Mr. Brooks." Her investigation would have to wait.

# 26 / DOOM AND GLOOM

At her fathers' request, Lemon left her entourage behind. She strolled into the familiar brownstone, where Patience awkwardly hovered over a sleeping baby, her tangled red hair dangling above Maria's face.

Lemon reached down to rub Widget's head but remained focused on her sister. "What are you doing?"

"I was tasked with keeping an eye on Maria," Patience said, still staring at the infant.

"I don't think—" Lemon let Patience be Patience and changed subjects. "This had better be good. I cancelled a show in Boston and lost two hundred followers."

"I postponed an investigation, as well as marital relations," Patience said with a slight smile.

"*Still?* Why the *florp* did you even get married?"

"I'm not certain," Patience said. "It seemed the correct thing to do after five dates."

Lemon slapped her own forehead.

Brooks and Smith trooped down the stairs. Smith was stone faced and Brooks tried to be, but he had a twitchy eye from all the stress.

"What are you doing?" Brooks asked Patience.

"Watching Maria," Patience said.

"That's not what—" His eye twitched again and he shook his head. "Just sit down. Both of you."

The girls seated themselves on one end of the couch. Smith and Widget joined them at the other end, and Brooks pulled a chair in close.

"We have a problem," Brooks said.

Lemon blurted a question. "Are you getting a divorce?"

"What? No." Brooks shook his head. "Why is that always your go-to?"

Smith chimed in. "We might be. Who knows?"

"Huh?" Lemon asked.

Brooks shut his eyes for a moment, until he was ready to put the information out. "Rhett Conner used a genie to change reality, and we're going to try to stop him and fix it."

"A genie?" Lemon giggled. She quickly stopped giggling. "You're serious."

Smith nodded. "Yeah. That was my reaction too."

Lemon eyed him with suspicion. "*You* giggled?"

"It was more of a guffaw..." Smith noted a look from his husband and shut himself up.

Brooks explained how Burroughs's analysis revealed a major change to reality, and how he and Smith had come to pin it on Rhett Conner. They couldn't explain much more than that because they didn't know much more than that.

"This explains why Ms. Darkstick hasn't returned home," Patience said. "We've been unable to contact her since she ventured to the Conner Building."

"Yeah, we don't care about that," Smith said.

"What are you gonna do with Rhett?" Lemon asked.

"Take away his geni—" Smith said.

"Kill him," Brooks said over him.

Lemon's eyes widened.

Smith tilted his head. "We're not *killing* him. Anyone could go a little power crazy with a genie. We just need to steal his lamp or whatever."

"He *messed with my head*," Brooks said.

"Probably on accident," Smith said. "I know you're a little wonky, but turn on some Ayne and calm down. You don't wanna kill anyone."

Brooks shook it off. "Yeah. You're right."

"What happens when you take the lamp back?" Lemon asked. "Do his wishes wear off?"

"That we don't know," Smith said.

"We don't know anything," Brooks said.

"Except some of what changed," Smith corrected.

Lemon tilted her head. "Such as?"

Brooks rattled off their list: the Empire State Building, Smith's face wound, Patience's marriage, Maria, Pop Tart & the Activation Energy—

At that, Lemon seized the conversation. "Why would Rhett Conner wish for any of that?"

"We don't know," Smith said. "My theory is... he's keeping us distracted."

"Or it could be secondhand effects from whatever he did wish for," Brooks said.

Lemon crossed her arms. "Do we get a say in this?"

"No," Brooks and Smith said.

"Wow," Lemon said.

"Sirs," Patience said. "Do you suppose it's possible you'll annul my marriage?"

"God, I hope so," Brooks said.

"Then I support your endeavor." Patience almost smiled. Then she recalled her earlier visit to the Connor Building. "How do you intend to reach Mr. Conner?"

"We made an appointment," Smith said. "They don't just let anyone up there."

"Yeah, they have some sort of advanced force field," Brooks said. "I thought you were working cases now..."

Patience lowered her head.

Lemon uncrossed her arms and re-crossed them in a huff. "You're gonna wreck my band."

Brooks snipped, "We don't know what's going to happen, but I'm glad your priorities are in the right place."

"What's it hurt if he has a genie?" Lemon asked.

Brooks looked for Smith to answer confidently.

"It might not hurt anything," Smith said. "But experience says it won't end well."

"So... a hunch?" Lemon said.

"It's our job to have a hunch," Smith said.

"Did you have a *hunch* you were gonna get shot in the face?" Lemon asked.

Smith shrugged. "If constant thoughts of impending doom count as a hunch. I told Brooksy things were too good and something bad would happen."

"Things are even better now," Lemon said.

"Exactly," Smith said. "Now I have another hunch."

Lemon groaned.

Brooks shook his head and tried to steer them back into more serious conversation. "Listen. It's like we said. Anything could happen, but we're going to investigate. We just wanted to make sure you both knew what was going on."

"What about Maria?" Lemon asked. "If you guys die, I can't take a baby on tour."

Smith answered. "Erin knows a couple. We already talked to her about making arrangements."

Patience took a modestly deep breath.

"What's wrong?" Brooks asked.

"I'd rather you didn't perish," Patience said.

"Uh... thanks. Us too," Brooks said.

"Please find Ms. Darkstick and return safely."

"We don't care about Darkstick," Smith said.

"*Please,*" Patience pleaded. Until she could get her marriage to disappear, she needed Susie at home to act as a clam jam.

"We'll try." Brooks turned to Lemon. "And we'll try not to ruin your band, if that's an option."

Lemon threw her fist out, and Brooks bumped it. The move filled her with confidence and filled him with worry. He and Smith were committed to this. They were going to march into the Conner Building and try to retrieve a genie.

They were idiots.

# 27 / SPIDER-MAN LOVES MARY JANE

"Never meet your heroes" is sound advice. "Never meet your villains" is even sounder advice, but is impractical when your villain holds power over the entire planet. So Brooks and Smith made their way to Rhett Conner's penthouse at the top of the Conner Building. The lobby had been empty, but the force field let them right through. At the end of a long, silent elevator ride, the two men paused outside a set of walnut double doors.

Brooks felt like he had to, so he started making a speech. "Whatever happens—"

Smith cut him off with a quick kiss. "I know."

Brooks scrunched his face at the interruption. "You don't."

"It's all that love shit. I know," Smith said.

"Charming," Brooks said. "But no."

Smith smirked. "You don't love me, then?"

Brooks sighed. "I just wanted you to know I'm sorry."

Smith's eyes darted from side to side. "For what?"

"For getting us into this," Brooks said.

Smith squinted. "You're sorry you figured out reality is fucked?"

"Yeah. I am. Whatever happens now is on me."

Smith stared into his eyes. He didn't have anything helpful to say, but before he could make an attempt, the doors opened inward. They each took a deep breath and stepped forward.

Inside was an idiot's vision of the billionaire lifestyle. Rhett greeted them in a royal purple robe with gold trim and gestured toward a small flight of stairs leading down into an impractical, below-floor sofa. At the square-shaped sofa's center was a fireplace and surrounding it sat ugly statues chosen for their expense rather than any artistic value. One was a carved walnut giraffe because of course it was.

The detectives made their way across the Calacatta marble floor and down the impractical stairs. They sat together, and Rhett seated himself perpendicular to them.

"Can I get either of you a drink?" he asked.

"No, thanks," Brooks said.

Smith shrugged and pointed at himself. "Alcoholic."

"That's too bad." Rhett clapped his hands twice to summon a hovertray that carried a bottle of expensive vegan cognac and three snifters. The tray landed next to him, and he served himself. "Imagin could fix that, if you want a sample dose."

"No thanks," Smith said.

Brooks muttered "tool" under his breath.

"How's business?" Rhett asked.

Smith glanced around the room and faked enthusiasm. "Not as good as yours."

"It's booming," Brooks said. "There's no end to the paranormal. That's why we're here."

Rhett smirked. "Getting right to it. What are you planning to do with this 'business expansion?'"

"The first thing is a tech refresh," Brooks lied. "We—"

"Rhett?" A whispery voice interrupted from across the room, where a busty brunette stood in a robe like Rhett's.

"I told you to wait," Rhett sneered.

"We've been waiting so long," the woman said.

From within the bedroom, a similar voice called out. "Come on, Rhett!"

"Get back in there," Rhett said. It was a threat.

The woman whimpered and retreated into the bedroom while Brooks and Smith shared a look of disgust.

"What happened to Solange?" Brooks asked.

Rhett leaned back and laughed. "Come on now. You didn't think I'd keep her around when I hit it big."

"I don't see why not," Brooks said. "Cute. Smart..." He wanted to add "willing to marry a douchebag," but stopped himself.

"Say you were me, and tomorrow you had billions," Rhett said. He gestured a thumb at Smith. "Are you really going to stay with a forty-year-old chunkster?"

Smith tried to find a problem with that statement. Not finding one, he shrugged.

Brooks folded his arms. "Yes."

"Why?" Rhett scoffed.

"Because I love that forty-year-old chunkster."

Smith spoke dryly. "Thanks, babe."

Rhett scoffed, "Love. Please."

"No, he really is into old dudes," Smith said. "I don't wanna get into how I know that, but..."

Brooks shot him a look, then continued interrogating Rhett. "So you divorced her."

"I wouldn't say *that*," Rhett chuckled.

Smith leaned forward, equally interested and disgusted. "Where's the genie?"

"The what?" Rhett asked, just barely feigning ignorance.

Smith had heard enough, and he sneered, "You *made your wife disappear*."

Brooks unfolded his arms and clenched his fists. "Okay, so we're doing this now..."

"You *Spider-Manned your wife*." Smith didn't mean to get into it so quickly, but he couldn't help himself. He turned to Brooks. "Sorry."

"It's fine," Brooks said. "Screw this guy."

Rhett chuckled and reached for his glass.

"Where's the damn genie, *Rhett*?" Smith asked.

Rhett took a sip and set the glass back down on his tray. He relished the detectives' discomfort as they waited.

After a drawn-out silence, Rhett's answer came with a SNAPP. With one quick flick of his middle finger and thumb, the entire room changed. Instead of being tucked in a penthouse, the recessed sofa occupied a small jungle clearing. Sounds of whispering playmates and clinking glasses gave way to chirping insects and a distant waterfall. A toucan flew overhead.

"I *am* the genie," Rhett said.

# 28 / PACIFISM

Sometimes, words fail. "Huh" wasn't a very good representation of the terror brought on by Rhett's revelation, but it was the only word that came to mind.

"Huh?" Brooks and Smith said at the same time.

"I'm the genie," Rhett said. "As you call it."

"Huh?" Smith said again.

Brooks tilted his head. "Three months ago you were *looking for* the genie."

"I was," Rhett said. "I found it."

"So you wished for it to make you into a genie too?" Brooks asked. It was a very Jafar thing to do.

"I'm confused," Smith said.

Rhett grinned. "You should be. I'm the only djinn expert in the world." He scooted closer to the detectives and attributed Solange's credentials to himself. She couldn't correct him, after all. "I studied them for close to a decade. What do you know about djinn?"

"It goes great with lime," Smith said.

Rhett ignored him.

"They grant wishes?" Brooks wondered.

"Not *quite*," Rhett said. "Djinn are superpowered beings like anything else the Reticent used to deal with. *Really* superpowered. Reality-bending stuff. See?" He snapped his fingers again, and the couch was in the middle of the Sahara.

Smith was too white for that. He groaned and raised an arm to shield himself from the sun. Rhett snapped his fingers again, and a giant beach umbrella staked itself into the sand to provide glorious shade for the entire couch.

"I take it there are no magic lamps either," Brooks said.

"Oh, you can trap them," Rhett tapped his bottle. "That's what I did."

Brooks blinked. "You put the genie in a cognac bottle?"

Rhett shrugged. "And a few flasks, a bottle of cologne, a barrel, a couple prescriptions... once you bottle it, there's no more physical entity. Just limitless creative energy. I take a sip, the bottle refills itself. Forever. It's so much better than 'granting wishes.' It's total control."

"You harvested a genie into LSD," Smith said.

Brooks frowned. "And you think you're the right person to wield that? Total control over everything?"

"I really do," Rhett said. "I have a vision. When—"

"We don't care," Brooks said.

Smith eyed Rhett. "I've gotta say... you're way more open about this than I expected."

Rhett laughed. "Well, you can't do anything about it. I love that. The two of you, living your lives, wondering whether anything that happens was because of me."

"So you messed with our lives for fun?" Brooks asked. That was what he'd been waiting for. A damned explanation for why their lives had changed.

Rhett didn't explain. Instead he squinted. "I haven't done *anything* to either of you, but I love that you think I did, because you guys are dicks."

"*We're* dicks?" Smith asked. "You *Spider-Manned your wife.*"

Brooks jumped up and darted for the cognac bottle. Rhett rolled his eyes and snapped his fingers. Brooks popped the bottle open and chugged. Nothing happened.

"I just did a bottle swap," Rhett said. "Sorry."

Brooks sulked back to his seat.

"You can try and kill me, but it won't work. You can try to get some of the djinn's essence. I won't let you. So let's just talk about your funding..."

Brooks grimaced. "What have you changed?"

"Again, nothing that concerns you. Really." Rhett pondered for a moment. "Well, I guess the extra paranormal activity affected you, but it wasn't *meant* for you."

"Who was it meant for?" Brooks asked.

"Does it matter? It's been great for your business."

"It *does* matter," Brooks said. "You think we *want* to live in a world where people get murdered by vampires every day? We do our job because we have to."

"Oh. Well in that case..."

Rhett snapped his fingers, and the group returned to his penthouse, sans the giant umbrella. "You're not going to need that funding."

"What?" Smith asked. "Why?"

"I just got rid of all superpowered beings."

"No way," Brooks said.

Rhett's eyes narrowed. "That should have included you. Weird."

Smith jumped off the couch, ready to hit someone named Rhett. "You were going to disappear *him*?"

"I'll disappear *you* if you don't watch your attitude." Rhett scratched at his nose. "You two need to leave. I'm done with you."

Smith was livid. "We don't need to do a damn—"

"We're leaving." Brooks roped an arm around Smith and walked with him to the door.

Smith looked back, red-faced. "That son of a—"

"*We're leaving.*"

# 29 / MOUTHLESS SCREAMS

In the paranormal detective line of work, death and disappearance were common—so much so that insurance companies created the Paranormal Death Index to calculate how likely employees at a given company were to perish, so they could adjust rates accordingly. ADHOC, for example, operated at a 0.02 PDI. That is, its employees had a two percent chance of dying in a given year. The Darkstick Agency's PDI, on the other hand, was 0.32. The difference between the two was mostly skill, but it was also partly luck. At any given moment, someone could be torn in half by a werewolf or choke on a curious fairy.

The effect of a genie encounter on PDI hadn't been calculated yet, but Patience guessed it had to put ADHOC above 0.50. So when Brooks and Smith filed through the front door of their home, Patience was relieved that her fathers had beaten the odds.

"Welcome home, sirs," Patience said.

Lemon checked her follower count and cheered. "I'm still successful!"

Widget jumped at Brooks's legs. Brooks leaned down and rubbed him.

Relief soon gave way to dismay, though not from Widget.

Patience looked down at her wedding band with a frown. "It appears I'm still married."

"You're still married because we didn't do a goddamn thing," Smith said.

He stomped across the room and took a seat near the girls, and Brooks did the same, minus the stomping. Widget hopped at Smith's legs, and he helped the undersized dog onto his lap.

"What happened?" Lemon asked.

"Rhett Conner doesn't *have* a genie. Rhett Conner *is* a genie," Brooks said.

"And he didn't kill you?" Lemon asked.

Smith pointed at Brooks, then back at himself. "Are we dead?"

"Guess not," Lemon said.

Patience had never stopped frowning, but her frown intensified. "I suppose I must go. Ms. Darkstick is still missing, and I can search for her in lieu of consummating my marriage."

"You can stay here if you want," Brooks said.

"Yeah, we can fix the marriage thing at the courthouse," Smith said. "You don't have to Spider-Man the guy—"

Brooks pursed his lips. "Would you stop with that?"

Patience shuffled toward the door. "No thank you, sirs. I promised I'd return home."

"We're gonna keep trying," Smith said. "Hang in there."

Patience began working the lace-up boots Susie bought her for Christmas. Each boot had twenty-three pairs of eyelets, so it would be a while.

Lemon wondered out loud, "But, like, how? How do you stop a genie?"

"No fucking clue," Smith said.

"Just... keep doing research, I guess," Brooks said.

"That sounds boring." Lemon stood and headed for the door, where Patience was halfway through lacing one boot. "I'm gonna go back on tour before you guys bork everything."

"Where are you playing next?" Smith asked.

"Hartford," Lemon said. She never bothered tying her sneakers, and she shoved her feet back into them. She looked down at Patience. "My chauffeur can drop you off first."

"I'd like that," Patience said.

Seeing Patience and Lemon in the doorway reminded Brooks how much was at stake. It was just him, Smith, and

Maria now. And if something were to happen to them—something like being genie-borked out of existence... He held on to the thought for the rest of the evening.

When the teenagers were gone and Maria was soundly asleep, Brooks and Smith retired to bed because that's what middle-aged people with babies do. There they began reminiscing, because that's also what middle-aged people with babies do.

"You remember that time you thought there was a changeling at the karaoke bar?"

Smith threw his back in embarrassment. "Yes. Fuck."

"On the bright side, that won't ever happen again." Brooks laughed.

Smith was tired and didn't follow. "Why?"

"All the vampires are gone," Brooks said. "All the wights. The wraiths. The changelings."

News reports confirmed what Rhett had done. The day's murder rate had fallen dramatically. Not one body drained of blood. Not one corpse dug up and maimed. Rhett took credit for it, of course, and soon a lengthy press conference with him filled their screen. Brooks grabbed the remote and muted him.

"Ugh. So what are we going to do?" Brooks asked.

"We're gonna figure out how to defeat Rhett," Smith said. "Research, like you said."

Brooks hesitated. "Still? I mean—"

Smith shook his head. "Come on, babe."

"I've been looking into it since we got home..."

Smith's head kept shaking. "No."

"Hear me out," Brooks said. "Bees were going extinct, which was an ecological disaster. So Rhett brought them back. He's been disappearing oil executives and members of the Walton family. And it turns out a lot of scientists are saying insects are a sustainable food source, so the spaghetti thing—"

"No. No. No." Smith couldn't fathom that Brooks needed to learn this lesson again.

Brooks continued. "On top of that, he just got rid of paranormal deaths. If Rhett had been a genie twelve years ago, my family would still be alive."

Smith rubbed at the inner corners of his eyes. "Fuck. Brooksy."

"I'm not saying he isn't a douche," Brooks said. "He deserves to die for what he did to Solange alone. But he's solving a lot of problems, and—"

"No."

"—and we *can't* defeat him, Eddie. So maybe we should just learn to love this world?"

"Just love it?" Smith asked.

"Yeah. Forget that it's been changed and just love it. For one thing, your past isn't as screwed up as it once was."

"I don't care," Smith said. "I'll take anything over being mind-fucked into Narnia."

"Trust me, you wouldn't."

"Trust me, I would. I'd rather know real pain than sit here wondering whether everything is made up or not." Smith summed up his lofty ideals: "It's about free will or some shit."

Brooks stared him down. He didn't necessarily want to hurt his husband, but he did want to make a point. "Do you remember who you lived with when you were nine years old?"

"What does that have to do with anything?" Smith asked.

"Do you?"

"Yeah. Tristan Gounaris. Guy beat the shit out of me and two other kids."

Brooks's voice got softer. "It wasn't just beating the shit out of you. Not originally."

"Okay." Smith caught his meaning. "So that's my life then. It's mine, and Rhett has no right to change it for worse *or better.* Besides, lots of kickass people got diddled and turned out just fine."

"What about the shooting?" Brooks noted. "You should be *dead.*"

"That's fine."

Brooks raised his voice. "That's *fine?*"

"If that's reality, yeah. That's fine. You of all people should get that," Smith said.

Brooks wasn't sure whether to be offended.

"And why's that?" he asked.

"Because I lived in your head for a while and it almost drove you bonkers? Because you're sitting on four sets of memories right now and it's driving you bonkers *again?* If we don't have control over our own bodies and minds, what the fuck do we have? What are we even fighting for?"

"*Nothing* now that all the monsters are dead," Brooks said. "Reality is whatever is happening right now. It doesn't matter how we got here."

"It always matters. Remember when you tried to change the timeline a few years ago and *died?*" Smith scooted closer and forced his frustration into compassion. "You were on the same page before. What happened?"

Brooks closed his eyes and took a deep breath. "I should have disappeared with all the other freaks, but I didn't."

"And that's bad because...?"

"Because. If Rhett can affect you and the girls but not me, I'd rather not mess with him." Brooks lowered his voice and spoke in a measured way. "I'm okay going down fighting. Yeah, free will. Great. But I'm not okay being the only survivor in my family *again.*"

"I don't want that to happen either, but you've said it yourself: this is bigger than us. He's already making people disappear," Smith said.

Brooks buried his head in his hands. "I can't *take* one more thing, Eddie."

"What do you mean?" Smith asked.

"It's driving me bonkers, like you said. I have *two timelines* in my head. I have *two sets of two timelines* in my head. All of my memories, *twice*. All of your memories, *twice*. And that's not counting all the extra cyborg perks. Did you know it's twenty-two degrees Celsius in this room right now? I do. Your heart's beating eighty-nine times per minute. The episode of *Gilligan's Butte* that's about to air is episode fifty-six. Spoiler: they don't get off the butte."

"I know it's hard," Smith said.

"*I feel like* you don't. How could you?"

"Because I couldn't do it. I thought the one timeline sucked bad enough that I killed myself, even without whatever bad memories I don't have anymore." Smith squinted, parsing whether the previous sentence meant what he intended. "But you're not me. You're—"

"What?" Brooks asked.

Smith struggled to find the right adverb. "You can handle it."

"I can't." Brooks frowned. "I..."

"What?" Smith asked.

Brooks spoke through his own fist. "I'm afraid of what me snapping looks like."

"I know you are," Smith said. "Woo-woo, remember?"

Brooks gave a despondent shrug. "I don't know what I'll do if everything is taken from me."

"I do," Smith said.

"What will I do, then?" Brooks asked.

"You'll survive."

Brooks groaned.

"I know you," Smith said. "I know you're stronger than you think, and I know you agree we have to take those genie powers away from Rhett."

"It doesn't matter what I believe. We *can't* do it, and we don't need to try."

"I wish you would listen to me," Smith said.
Brooks's mouth disappeared.

# 30 / FUN TIMES WITH GENIE POWERS

Reliving every newfound-superpower montage he'd ever seen, Smith leapt from the bed and paced.

"Holy shit. Holy shit. Holy shit," he said.

Brooks tapped at his face with a look of panic in his eyes.

"Uh... I wish you had a mouth again," Smith said.

With his newly restored mouth, Brooks asked an important question in a language Smith was comfortable with. "What the fuck, Eddie?"

Smith didn't answer that. Instead, he ignored his lofty assertion that he wouldn't use genie powers, instead fulfilling his promise to wish for frivolities on a whim.

"I wish I was wearing a hat," Smith said. A *Make America Great Again* hat appeared on his head. He pulled it off, cringed, and tossed it. "Not that hat." It morphed into a fedora on the floor. "Uh... I wish I had a foot-long dick." He pulled the waist of his pajama pants out and looked inside. "You're gonna love this."

"I'm... I..." Brooks hopped off the bed and approached Smith with a quizzical face. "Are you a genie?"

"I dunno. *Apparently*."

Brooks folded his arms. "*Apparently*? Did you get into Rhett's drink, or...?"

"I wish Anderson Cooper was here," Smith said.

The silver-haired journalist appeared, confused. Before he could ask any of the five Ws, Smith registered Brooks's disapproval and sent him back to whatever disaster-torn nation he came from.

"Eddie—"

"I wish for a taco," Smith said. When a taco appeared in

his hand, he grinned.

*Limitless creative energy.* That's what Rhett said, and it was what Smith was throwing out into the universe. He discarded his freewill principles faster than the chastity pledge he made at Jesus Camp '88.

Brooks blinked, speechless as Smith took a bite of his taco.

Smith swallowed, then pointed at Brooks's face. "I wish he had a mustache."

"I wish you would take this seriously," Brooks said, bristling.

Smith's smile disappeared and he looked contrite. "You're right. I'm sorry."

"*A la verga,*" Brooks said. Did he have powers too? That wasn't right. He hesitated for a moment, trying to come up with something harmless. "I... wish for three hundred dollars."

The money appeared on the bed in front of him.

"Oh, no," Brooks said.

Smith's eyes widened. "I wish you didn't have three hundred dollars."

The money disappeared.

"I wish I did," Brooks said.

The money reappeared, smoking a little from being pulled into and out of existence.

Smith's posture improved from excitement. "Ooh. I've got it. I wish Rhett would disappear."

On screen, a muted Rhett continued blathering about his achievements.

"Damn," Smith said, returning to a slouch. "I thought that might work."

"You're onto something. He couldn't make me disappear. Remember?"

"All three of us are genies?" Smith wondered.

"How? Just... how? We didn't drink any of his magic juice. Did we?"

"No," Smith said. He looked at a nightstand and snapped his fingers. A pristine, mint grade copy of *Action Comics* #1 appeared. "Hey, I don't even have to say 'I wish.'"

"You..." Brooks took a seat at the foot of the bed and slouched. "*Oh God.*"

"What?" Smith asked.

Brooks thought hard, not even bothering to snap his fingers. A new bassinet appeared in the room with a new screaming baby.

"Ugh. Make it go away," Smith said.

The mystery baby disappeared, and Smith had the same realization Brooks just had. He seated himself next to his husband. "Oh..."

"Oh, God," Brooks repeated. "We could have done anything. How the hell did this happen? How long have we been able to do this?"

"I don't know," Smith said.

Many people dream of influencing the world, but not many dream having no clue they've been doing so. If Brooks and Smith gained this ability in the last day, that was one thing. If they'd gained it a few months earlier, it was quite another.

"How far do you think this goes?" Smith asked.

"Like, how many people are genies?" Brooks raised his hands in an I-give-up gesture.

"Well the good news is, if Rhett murders one of us, the other can bring them back."

"You think we can bring people back from the dead?" Brooks asked.

"Oh... uh... no," Smith said. He knew exactly which massacred family Brooks would try to bring back. "Don't do it."

"Why not?" Brooks asked.

"Because we're going to un-genie ourselves and anyone else as soon as we figure out how. Then your dead family's gonna die *again* and you're gonna freak out even more."

"Yeah, good point." Brooks still wanted to do it, but he

restrained himself. "What if we didn't un-genie ourselves, though?"

"Christ. One is bad enough, you think *we* should be allowed to change everything?"

"I think we already did," Brooks said.

"Well, R.E.M. and Burt Bacharach were probably us," Smith said.

"Yeah, probably. Do you think..." Brooks wouldn't let himself finish the question.

"Do I think you willed Maria into existence and made me forget about it?" Smith asked.

Brooks glared. "Well. Good to know where your mind is."

Smith tented his fingers. "I'm thinking we need to figure out what we did, what Rhett did, what anybody else did, and what was supposed to happen on its own."

"Genie interference exists—obviously—so how can we know what was supposed to happen without it?" Brooks asked.

"I don't know. We're gonna need all your sets of memories, that's for sure."

Brooks rested his head in his hand. He caught most of the tears, but a small stream made it down the side of his face.

"Whoa. Hey, it's not that bad." Smith willed a cookie bouquet into existence and handed it over.

"I don't want a cookie bouquet, Eddie," Brooks said. The bouquet disappeared.

"Come on." Smith brought it back. Just as the pile of money had, the bouquet smoked a little.

"No." Annoyed, Brooks disappeared it again.

"Well, I'm gonna have some," Smith said. But he couldn't. When he recreated the cookie bouquet, it was completely engulfed in flames. He jumped backward. "I wish that wasn't on fire."

Nothing happened.

"I wish that weren't on fire," Brooks said, as if the

improper subjunctive was what caused Smith's request to fail.

Nothing happened, except that their bedspread also caught fire.

"I wish I had a fire extinguisher," Brooks and Smith said.

One appeared for each of them, and they extinguished the flames.

"Okay," Brooks said. "You're right. This could be way more dangerous than I thought."

Smith didn't hate to say his next words: "*I told you so.*"

# 31 / STICK IT BACK

It turns out waltzing into a genie's building to accuse him of stealing your genie isn't a great idea. Susie Darkstick ruminated on that as she stood chained to a wall in the Conner Building. Rhett, still wearing his robe, glowered at her. When she had first entered the lobby and shouted "Genie! Are you in here?" at the force field, Rhett laughed and let her upstairs to have another laugh. When she accused him of having a genie to his face, he'd laughed and snapped them into the jungle, just like he had for Brooks and Smith. But when she told Rhett that he'd stolen his powers from her genie and demanded that he give it back, he tied her up and began interrogating her.

"Where did you find a djinn?" he asked.

Susie growled. "You'll never make me talk, Conner."

Rhett sighed, snapped his fingers, and removed the oxygen from the air around her. Susie flailed and spluttered. Her face turned blue. When Rhett snapped the oxygen back, she was more compliant.

"Fine. I'll talk," Susie choked. Her kids loosely needed her.

"Where did you find a djinn?" Rhett asked again.

Susie cleared her throat. "I was walking around Central Park, investigating my late husband's death. I hadn't ruled out the possibility of mutant snails crawling into people's brains, so I knelt down on the sidewalk to check under a rock. There weren't any snails, but there was a small amulet shaped like a lamp. When I got home, I rubbed it and a genie popped out. The rest is history."

"No, the rest isn't history," Rhett said. "I want to know more."

"Well, first I wished to bring my husband back to life, but the genie couldn't do that. So I wished for some money to get my business off the ground..."

"I don't care what you wished for," Rhett said.

"I don't know anything else," Susie said.

"What you're describing *isn't how djinn work*. It's not how they're supposed to work, anyway. Did it say why it was granting you wishes?"

"It congratulated me for finding it," Susie said.

Rhett groaned. "What did it look like?"

"Like a genie. You know... blue, cloudy..."

"Like in *Aladdin*?" Rhett asked.

"Yeah, exactly," Susie said.

"Okay, you're messing with me."

"I'm not," Susie said. "In any case, why does it matter? You stole my genie and its powers, and I want it back."

Rhett paced the room. "First of all, I didn't steal some blue cartoon *genie*. I encountered and bottled a dangerous djinn. And it matters because it's *not working*."

"What do you mean?" Susie asked. "You just used it to asphyxiate me."

"I tried to kill you, but I couldn't. Sometimes I just can't do things. It's like the power is fighting me. If this thing is somehow loyal to you, I want to know why, and I want to know how to make it stop."

"What else did you try to do that didn't work?" Susie asked.

"Nice try," Rhett said. "I'm not telling you what I want to do with my powers so you can use your connection to the djinn to stop me."

Susie pouted. "Fine. I'll just stand here then."

"Yeah. You will. Until you decide to be useful."

Something about the way Rhett said that gave Susie pause. Whatever he wanted her to be 'useful' for couldn't be anything good.

# 32 / MAKING A LIST, CHECKING IT TWICE

Brooks and Smith had found themselves living in a post-reality world. With at least three people manipulating life into what they wanted it to be, they had no way of sorting out the way things were *supposed* to be. They could have gotten on Twitter and started hashtagging #FakeReality, but Smith had already used his power to make Twitter disappear, and Brooks had taken no issue with that. Somewhere in Connecticut, though, Lemon was distraught.

The detectives relocated to Smith's downstairs office and got to work with pencils and notepads. It was finally the perfect opportunity for Smith to create a crazy wall, and he was going to seize it by refusing to digitize. Their mission was to figure out who changed what and agree on what they wanted to keep from their current reality and what they wanted to revert. Once they had lists, everything would be festooned to the wall. Smith had green and orange yarn at his side, ready to go.

"So the good news," he said, "is we agreed on Maria or she would have combusted."

"Yeah," Brooks said. It was a pretty low bar for good news.

In the corner of the room, Maria lay in her bassinet, staring at her hands and smiling for no reason. In the middle of the room, the detectives were trying to jot down all the things they may have willed into or out of existence.

"I don't have a problem with the Empire State Building, do you?" Smith asked.

"No. I'd say that was Rhett, since he built his building where it used to be."

Smith made an addition to his Rhett column:

| ME | BROOKSY | RHETT |
|---|---|---|
| BACHARACH | REM | ~~SOLANGE~~ |
| GILLIGAN? | MARIA | BEES |
| 12" COCK | ADHOC $$$ | SPAGHETTI |
| ~~TWITTER~~ | NICE WEATHER? | ~~WOO WOO DOC~~ |
| | | EMPIRE STATE |

Brooks's list was a bit more worrisome, both because it
was longer and because his handwriting looked like a com-
mand line font.

| Rhett | Eddie | Me |
|---|---|---|
| Money | NOT DYING | Maria |
| Success | NO FACE WOUND | R.E.M. |
| Fame | XL Penis | PT&TAE? |
| Dead Wife | Cookie bouquet | ADHOC success |
| Dead Therapist | "Raindrops..." | Dead Zane |
| Harem | Parents in NJ? | |
| Bees | Burroughs' hair? | |
| ESB | | |
| Extra para- | | |
| normal activity, | | |
| then NONE | | |
| Spaghetti | | |
| Nice weather? | | |

Smith looked down at their sleeping dog. "What about
Wid-get?"

"Both of us, I guess," Brooks said.

"We're definitely keeping Widget, right?"

"Yes." Brooks scribbled the dog's name onto his list. "We
have to be careful. If one of us wants something and the
other doesn't... who knows? Maybe we did the Empire State
Building in by having an argument."

"Right, we try to make opposites happen... kaboom. That's probably why Rhett couldn't kill you. You didn't want to die." Smith had an idea. "But what if we *both* want him de-powered?"

Brooks's eyes widened. "Two outnumbers one."

Smith did his best Captain Planet voice. "By your powers combined—"

"Stop it," Brooks said.

"Yeah, okay." Smith huffed. "It might work, though."

"We just have to agree on everything," Brooks said.

"Can't be that hard," Smith said.

A knock at the front door was about to make it hard. While Brooks tried to figure out who would have wanted Patience married off, Smith got up to answer.

"I'll get it," he said.

Smith expected Mormons or Girl Scouts now that they sold cookies throughout the year (and he made a mental note that this was probably his doing). Instead, he greeted a man and woman in their mid-sixties and another woman in her mid-thirties. Judging from their faces, the younger one was the daughter of the other two. They were familiar to Smith, but he couldn't quite place them.

"Can I help you?" he asked.

"Could you tell me if Arturo lives here?" the man asked.

"Um, why?" Smith asked. He made it a rule not to trust strangers who appeared at his door asking about his husband. It wasn't something that happened often enough to deserve a rule, but it was a rule nonetheless.

The man hit Smith with a look that was both puzzled and annoyed. A puzzled and annoyed look Smith had seen hundreds of times before. He had an awful realization. The three people in front of him were the aged-up members of the formerly dead Brooks family: Norman, Maria, and Tasha. Just thinking about a world where they'd never died had created that world. This was bad.

"No." Smith shook his head. "No. You need to go away."

"I'm sorry?" Norman asked.

Brooks called out from inside. "You okay?"

Smith repeated himself in a lower voice. "Go away."

Just as Brooks walked over to investigate, his family disappeared into thin air. Smith shut the door on the vanishing Brookses.*

"What was that?" Brooks asked.

"Nothing. Just Mormons."

Brooks was both puzzled and annoyed. "So you made them disappear? I know you're not a big fan, but you could have just told them to leave."

Smith's eyes darted around as he tried to decide on a lie.

Brooks glowered at him. "*Eddie?*"

"Don't be mad," Smith said, knowing Brooks would be mad.

"I can't promise that." Brooks shook his head. "What did you do?"

Smith blurted the truth. "It was your dead family."

"*WHAT?*" Brooks put his hands on Smith's shoulders and shook them. "What the *hell* were you thinking? *All of them?*"

Smith grabbed the hands and removed them, as delicately as he could while still letting his husband know he was annoyed. "We *both* agreed that seeing them would just hurt you more when they had to disappear, so I just... made it so you wouldn't have to see?"

"How could you do that?" Brooks asked.

Smith blinked. "With genie powers?"

"That's not funny, and it's not fair," Brooks said. "How could you do that *to me?*"

"You know what isn't fair?" Without missing a beat, Smith answered his own question. "Apparating a baby into our

---

* The Vanishing Brookses was also the name of a Des Moines family's circus act, until they all vanished.

lives."

"We *agreed*."

"And we *agreed* you wouldn't bring your family back to life. But there they were." Smith put a hand to his chin. "Almost like you don't care what we *agree to*."

"I didn't do it on purpose. Just like you didn't start Burt Bacharach on purpose. Things just happen. But my family showed up and you murdered them."

"No. They got murdered a long time ago," Smith said. "Let me get this straight. It's a huge deal if you have to use your cyborg powers to break doors or scan the internet, but using magic genie powers to resurrect your family is hunky-dory?"

"Yes. Because I don't want to be a cyborg." Brooks wasn't just beating a dead horse at this point; he was committing a hate crime against one.

"Oh, really?" Smith's voice was heavy with sarcasm. "I had no idea."

Brooks responded with his most intimidating stance. "I want to see them."

The knock at the door returned, and Smith moved in front of it. He didn't have an intimidating stance, but he tried.

"No. Stop it," Smith said.

"Eddie, you know I'd never hit you, but I really want to right now."

"Tough," Smith said. He thought hard and the knocking stopped mid-knock.

"Stop willing my family away," Brooks said.

"Stop willing them back to life," Smith said.

Brooks mocked Smith's earlier sentiment. "Can't be that hard to agree on things."

"Fine. Wish them back," Smith said. "I don't care. Spend the whole week with your family and *then* watch them disappear. Hell, spend a year with them. That'll be better. Fuck it. Everyone wish for everything!" He threw up his hands. "I wish for the Nile!"

"You can't have the Nile," Brooks said.

"Sure I can, if you can have your dead parents."

Smith thought hard, trying to make the Nile appear. Brooks, meanwhile, thought hard to prevent it. The ground beneath them trembled, and every non-secured object in the house began rattling at once. One picture of the family fell from the wall and shattered. Widget took an alarmed stance and barked a long, uninterrupted string of barks. From the office, Maria wailed.

Their parental instincts took over, and Brooks and Smith rushed toward the office, even as they kept arguing.

"You can't have the damn Nile," Brooks said.

"I don't want it anyway," Smith said as the ground stilled. "I was trying to make a point."

In her bassinet, Maria was just fine. Smith's illogically calming presence did its thing as he picked her up and rocked her.

"What point?" Brooks asked.

"We just caused an earthquake," Smith said.

Brooks slouched a bit, acquiescing.

Smith reiterated, "*We're* the danger this time. Us, and Rhett, and anyone else who might be out there using genie magic to stuff heads in toilets and drop lighting fixtures."

"I know." Brooks shook his head and softened his tone. "I know. I'm just frustrated. What if it turns out there are a thousand Rhetts? If they all get to use genie powers for their benefit, so should we. Haven't we earned it?"

"No, babe. You'd be hard pressed to find anyone who's earned that. A thousand Rhetts does sound like a nightmare, though." Smith sighed. "Uh... I wish we knew what we were up against?"

Nothing happened.

"That right there," Brooks said. He gesticulated as he aired another grievance. "If our power is unlimited, why don't some things work? Why can I bring back my family, but you can't get basic information?" He watched Maria grasp at

Smith's shirt. "Why can we *create a child* but not stop Rhett? It's supposed to be unlimited creative energy, right?"

"Honestly, it feels like we're being manipulated," Smith said.

"It does, doesn't it?" Brooks asked.

Smith's eyes widened and he bit his lip. He remembered something. Something manipulative.

"You have an idea?" Brooks asked.

"I think so."

Smith did, but it was a stupid idea.

# 33 / DONNA!

One thing hadn't changed in the last three months: *Donna!* was still America's number one daytime talk show. The chubby, enthusiastic host brought millions joy with everything from paternity test reveals to frank discussions on coping with newfound superpowers. She also lavished her in-studio audience with fabulous swag. On this day, they received go-karts.

"This is the stupidest idea you've ever had," Brooks said.

"That's saying something," Smith said.

"Yeah. It is."

Smith had remembered the TV at Tiffany's and how its ad seemed made for them. Having answered the casting call for cyborgs who died, they relaxed backstage next to a bowl of green-only M&Ms and a crate of sparkling water. With plush chairs and an absence of people snorting coke, the accommodations were a lot nicer than the last place they went backstage. But Pop Tart & the Activation Energy doing lines off each other was more interesting than the in-studio monitor that displayed a live feed of the show they were about to participate in.

On screen, a man and woman argued. The husband, Bernie, wore a short-sleeved button down shirt with a snake on it that was undoubtedly the nicest shirt he owned. The wife, Shari, wore a too-tight sequined t-shirt that exposed both the bottom of her stomach and the top of her ass. Both sat on a long, blue couch, facing the host, who was parked in her signature armchair. At the bottom of the screen, the words 'My Baby Daddy Is an Alien' described the couple's problem.

"I don't care what your dee-en-ayy says. That baby is mine," Bernie shouted. "He has my eyes!"

"He's got three of 'em," Shari said, looking down at the

infant in her arms.

Baby Goobert, distressed from his parents' arguing, began to wail and flail his tentacle.

"Don't mean he's no alien," Bernie said. "It's a genetic dee-fect."

Shari's head pecked forward like a bird as she told him how it was. "I slept with a alien, Bernie. You's just gonna have to accept that."

"I don't gotta do *nothin*," Bernie said. He rose to leave the stage, but a large, angry bodyguard wasn't having it, and intimidated him back into position.

"We'll be right back," Donna! said.

Backstage, a production assistant tapped on the door and entered. "Okay. You two are up next."

"How?" Smith asked. "They're not done with their alien thing yet."

Brooks squinted. "They save all the resolutions for the end. You've never watched this show?"

"You *have*?" Smith asked.

Brooks tried way too hard to lie. "*No*... I mean, I know it because of research..."

Smith popped a few green M&Ms. "Uh huh."

They made their way out the door and into a hallway filled with awards and framed magazines bearing Donna!'s face.

Brooks explained himself further. "I've only seen it in passing when I'm home with Maria."

"That's weird," Smith said. "When I stay home and watch her, *I* don't lose my sense of taste."

"You don't *have* a sense of taste," Brooks said.

"You really want to go down that rabbit hole?" Smith asked.

Brooks huffed. "*Fine.*"

Soon they stood at the edge of the stage, awaiting their cue. Donna!'s introduction wasn't quite audible from their vantage point, but the headphone-wearing assistant had no trouble. With a gesture they were sent on their way.

"...uro Brooks and Edward Smith!"

The room was completely silent. As it turned out, the 'live studio audience' promised at the beginning of every episode was a combination of laugh track and stock footage added in post-production. The swag was a lie, and if Brooks and Smith had actually read the non-disclosure agreement they signed, they would have known they were never allowed to mention it. They awkwardly made their way across the stage and parked themselves on a long blue couch next to the alien family. Bernie coughed a little.

Donna!'s chair was set at an angle from the couch. She played to the nonexistent audience by looking their way and throwing out her hands. "From aliens to cyborgs, how about that?" Applause would be added later. For now, Brooks and Smith blinked and waited for their turn to speak.

"Arturo, you're a cyborg," Donna! said. "Is that right?"

"Yeah," Brooks said.

She leaned in to show sensitivity. "And how did that happen?"

"Uh, I died and my company brought me back to life," Brooks said.

"How does that make you *feel?*" Donna! asked.

Brooks stared at her. "Uh, not great."

Donna! nodded. "Interesting. Interesting. This is your husband, right?"

"Yeah," Brooks and Smith said.

"Eddie," Donna! said. "How has this change affected your marriage?"

"Uhh..." Smith pinched a finger over his mic, leaned in, and whispered into Brooks's ear. "What is she doing?"

"She's doing her show," Brooks whispered back.

"I thought this whole thing was a trap for us. I didn't actually come up with anything to say."

"I don't know," Brooks said. "Be trashy."

Donna! repeated herself. "How has this change affected your marriage, Eddie?"

"I'll tell you how!" Smith said, affecting a Southern accent. "We cain't have sex no more!"

Donna! paused so the audience could later gasp. "And why is that?"

Brooks shut his eyes and braced for stupidity.

Smith continued. "He's got himself a cold robo-dick. It's like suckin' on a spoon someone left in the icebox."

"Wow," Brooks said, his astonishment genuine.

"How does that make *you* feel?" Donna! asked Brooks.

"Um..." Brooks pretended to wipe away a tear. "It's hurtful, you know? I may have a robo-dick, but I'm still a human being."

There was a pause for "aww" noises before Donna! continued. "Is it true that—"

She looked up toward a slight creaking sound that became a THUNK. Like that, Donna! was the victim of yet another falling lighting fixture.

Shari clutched her alien baby tight and turned away, while stagehands gasped and shrieked and called for help.

"Got damn," Bernie said. "Y'all ever seen sumpin' like that?"

Brooks groaned. "Yes. Yes we have."

Smith eyed the spreading pool of blood. "*Fucking again?*"

"Well, it was a message, all right," Brooks said.

"Not one from Donna!, though," Smith said.

They were lost, again.

# 34 / IMPROVISATION

Annoyed with each other, annoyed with *Donna!*, and annoyed that none of their research ever seemed to go anywhere, Brooks and Smith genied themselves back to the top of the Conner Building, where Rhett—they assumed—had a message for them. They went in without formalizing a plan.

Smith burst through the door first. "Why did you have to kill Donna!?"

Rhett was sipping champagne on his couch. "How did you two get up here? What are you talking about?"

"Randomly crushed by a lighting fixture?" Brooks asked. "*Really?*"

"Who's Donna?" Rhett asked.

"Donna!!" Brooks said. "The talk show host. Big deal. Has a book club? *Had* a book club..."

Rhett tilted his head. "Why would I kill a talk show host?"

"That's what we're asking," Smith said.

"I didn't, so..." Rhett dismissed them with a sweeping gesture. "Go away. I'm busy solving climate change."

Smith glowered at him. "No. You're not the only genie in this room, asshole."

Rhett set his drink down. "Excuse me?"

The element of surprise was all they had, and Brooks seized it. He wished for Rhett to be crushed under a lighting fixture, and—sure enough—one appeared from nowhere to crush him. The cracking and smushing sounds seemed to say their problem was solved.

Smith's jaw dropped. "Jesus, Brooksy. I thought we were gonna depower him."

Before he could fully freak about the murder, the lighting fixture disappeared and Rhett stood in its place, perfectly healthy.

"That's funny," Rhett said. "It doesn't work that way, but it's funny you think it does."

Brooks sneered. "*What?*"

"Djinn can't use their powers to harm other djinn. You have powers?" Rhett brushed it off. "That's fine."

"Fuck," said Smith.

Rhett smirked. "And what's more..."

Seldom has anything good ever followed the words "what's more." The first recorded use of the phrase occurred in 1814, when George III ordered an execution. In his decree, the king said, "You will be hanged. What's more, your body will be left until it is nothing but bones. What's more, those bones will be ground to ash and set on the floor of my bedchamber, so that they may absorb any leavings of my tipped chamberpot. You have acted against the crown. And what's more, your descendants will defame the throne by placing my name on a Wikipedia article entitled 'List of mentally ill monarchs.'" He was right about the article. Still, it wasn't good news for the people of the time, who took it to mean their king—who suffered acute time-sickness—was out of his mind.

Rhett, as expected, followed "what's more" with bad news. He took a few steps toward the detectives. "I *can* hurt *you*."

"You just said genies can't hurt other genies," Smith said.

"I did," Rhett said. "I called us *djinn*, but yes."

"So you're a liar?" Brooks asked.

Rhett smirked. "Sometimes. Not right now, though."

Without explaining himself further, Rhett summoned Lemon, Patience, and Maria to the room.

Lemon didn't notice the change in scenery. Though Twitter was gone, there was plenty to keep her absorbed in her phone. Patience froze in fear at the edge of the recessed couch. Maria did nothing, because she was a baby.

"I could kill *any one of them*, and you couldn't do anything about it," Rhett said.

Lemon finally looked up. "Huh? What's this *feckler* doing here?"

With a finger snap, Patience and Maria disappeared, and Lemon dropped to the floor, dead. She fell face down, exposing the back of her jacket, which read: PT&TAE 2017 TOUR.

Brooks snapped his fingers and wished her back to life. Nothing happened.

Smith did the same, to the same result. "What the hell?"

Brooks knelt down next to Lemon and looked up at Rhett, spitting mad. "Where are the other two?"

"I put them back where I found them," Rhett said.

Smith knelt down next to Brooks and began snapping his fingers and wishing Lemon back. "Come on, genie powers."

Brooks rolled Lemon over, and the reality of the situation hit them. Her eyes—normally vibrant with hipster snark—had nothing behind them. Her lips were pale. The girl who'd been a huge part of their lives for two years was gone. Gone for no other reason than Rhett proving a point. Brooks let himself sit on the floor, and he put a hand on Lemon's cheek.

*It's happening again*, he thought.

Smith, meanwhile, snapped and snapped. Nothing changed.

"Oh," Rhett said. "Fun fact. You can't reverse another djinn's magic, either."

Smith objected, remembering Burt Bacharach, the pile of money, the mystery baby, the Nile, and Brooks's family. "That's not tr—"

Brooks nudged him quiet and spoke softly. "Something's weird and he doesn't know it."

"Bring her back," Smith demanded.

Rhett chuckled. "No."

Brooks looked up and pleaded. "Please."

"She didn't do anything to you," Smith said.

"You have no bargaining power," Rhett said. "What can

you offer me that I can't create for myself? Nothing. But I bet you'll leave me alone now."

Smith put a hand on Lemon's shoulder, shut his eyes, and focused as hard as he could on resurrection. Brooks forced himself back up onto his knees, then to his feet.

"I wish Rhett was on fire," Brooks said.

Smith's eyes shot open. "What the fuck?"

Rhett caught fire, but it didn't harm him.

Brooks stared at Rhett as he wished for his death. "I wish he was on Mars."

That didn't work at all.

"I wish he didn't have lungs. I wish he didn't have legs. I wish he was drowning. I wish his throat was slit."

As Brooks sobbed and rambled, the penthouse floor shook beneath them. Rhett, like most people, didn't want to bleed to death or drown. His desires clashed with Brooks's, putting the universe in jeopardy again.

"Stop it," Smith said. "We need to leave."

"*Do we now?* You were all for charging in here and stopping him. Now Lemon's dead, and for what? We haven't changed *anything.*"

"We'll fix it," Smith said. "We'll figure out the catch and fix it. But we can't do that if we break the whole world in half. Patience and Maria are still waiting for us."

Rhett wished for the Conner Building to stabilize itself; Brooks wished it would collapse. A sound more horrible than BLOOOOORN came from the building's foundation—the sound of folding metal and collapsing concrete. Beneath them, a crack spread across the penthouse floor. Brooks instinctively reached for Lemon, but the gap widened and claimed her body, along with some pieces of furniture. Brooks and Smith fell backward and held onto each other.

"Let's just wish we were back home," Smith said.

"I don't want to be home. I don't want to be anywhere."

Smith's desire for Brooks countered Brooks's desire to

disappear, and the building shook harder. The Conner Building's unbreakable windows gave out and sprayed shattered glass across the floor. One sharp piece wedged into the back of Smith's arm. He wished it away and shook his arm.

"Brooksy, *come on.* Let's go home."

"I can't."

"You can." Smith looked at Brooks with glassy eyes. "Count of three. One—"

"Heeeeeeelp!" called a female voice from below.

From the depths of the Conner Building's gaping hole, Brooks and Smith could hear screaming several floors below.

Brooks shook himself back into action. "Maybe we can still save someone."

"Good. Perfect. Let's go," Smith said. He didn't care what they did, so long as it got them away from Rhett and kept Brooks too busy to wallow in despair.

The building buckled and creaked. Brooks and Smith stumbled across the broken, canted marble and reached the door.

Rhett—floating peacefully in a lotus position—snipped at them. "Good. Go. Bother me again and I'll kill the other two." Then he mumbled something grumpy about having to rebuild, even though it would require zero physical effort on his part.

Brooks and Smith rushed out of the room and headed for the emergency stairs, dodging marble tiles and broken handrails as the stairwell waved and collapsed around them. At the next floor, they opened the door and poked their heads into an empty hallway.

"Not this one," Smith said.

A piece of falling debris nearly concussed Smith, but Brooks yanked him out of the way.

"We can do this the easy way," Brooks said. His eyes pulsed red for a moment as he activated his ability to scan for life. "There's no one on the next two floors," he said and pulled Smith down the stairs.

They didn't stop to think about how peculiar it was for multiple floors of a skyscraper to lie empty. They didn't stop to think about anything. One critical part of being a paranormal detective was using the job to mask pain and frustration. The sadder the life, the greater the satisfaction in saving a life. And Brooks and Smith were miserable.

That was great news for Susie Darkstick. Brooks and Smith burst into the room where Susie remained handcuffed to a wall.

Smith threw up his hands. "Fuck. You didn't say it was her."

"I didn't know." Brooks scowled. "I wish she were free, I guess."

Susie's bonds disappeared, and she affected her deep voice. "Thanks."

"Do we have to take her with us?" Smith asked.

"I have valuable information," Susie said. "But you'll need to get me out of here first."

Brooks sighed. There was no way Susie knew anything of value.

Smith looked to Brooks. "Okay. Now. Wish to be home in 3... 2... 1..."

# 35 / EXCITING NEW WAYS TO SUFFER

Two and a half detectives appeared in Brooks and Smith's living room. Susie beelined for a nearby shelf and began checking out family photos and knick-knacks. She eyed pictures of the girls in particular.

"Oooh, what are their names?" Susie asked.

"Go home," Brooks said.

She spotted the bassinet with a sleeping Maria inside it and scurried to it while making a high-pitched, ovary-driven sound.

"Touch her and I will stab you," Brooks said.

Smith glanced at him with a sinking feeling.

Susie wasn't disturbed. She simply tapped her tape recorder and narrated. "The detectives are touchy about their family. I wonder what happened."

Brooks raised his voice and ranted. "What happened is Rhett Conner murdered one of our daughters and threatened to do the same to the other two. We have genie powers, but we can't reverse his magic because nothing makes any sense. Now I'm ready to snap and—" He pointed at Smith. "—he's bound to go on a depressed bender any minute now. Okay? You all up to speed?"

Susie tucked into her shoulders. "O... kay."

"I'm not gonna go on a bender," Smith mumbled.

"I'm sorry for your loss," Susie said.

Brooks cracked up. "Can it, Darkstick."

Smith, for a change, tried to focus. "Why did he have you tied up?"

"I started asking uncomfortable questions," growled Susie.

"About?" Smith asked.

Brooks rolled his eyes at the notion of entertaining Susie Darkstick.

Smith just tried to keep the conversation going. He had to keep it going, because whatever came after would be worse. He rephrased his question. "What did you ask him?"

Susie smirked. "Maybe we can help each other."

"No," Brooks said.

"I want my genie back," she said, "and you want to punish Rhett Conner."

Brooks rolled his eyes. "There is nothing you can help us with, okay?" He turned back to Smith. "We can reverse each other's magic, but not Rhett's. Why?"

Susie cleared her throat. They ignored it.

"I don't know," Smith said. "There's a hierarchy, maybe? Based on who got their powers first?"

Susie cleared her throat louder.

"*What?*" Brooks snapped.

"You're not genies," Susie said.

"Oh, really?" Brooks asked. He snapped his fingers and the living room walls changed from gray to green. He snapped them again to change from green to blue. "Tell me more."

"You're not genies," Susie repeated. "The genie's fighting back through you."

Brooks and Smith stared at her with dumbfounded looks.

Susie sat down and tried to pet Widget, who was having none of that. "While Rhett had me captive, he tried to make me disappear. It didn't work. I think because the genie didn't want to kill its former master. Anyway, he started ranting and raving about the genie not giving him one hundred percent of its power." She finally had their attention. "It doesn't accept Rhett. It can't hurt him since he took its power, but even as essence it still has some power over the world. Over its own destiny."

"Donna! *was* a message," Smith said. "But not from

Donna! or Rhett. The genie was trying to get our attention that something was wrong... it's probably what borked your backup in the first place, so we'd realize."

Brooks shook his head. "Lighting fixtures crushing people... heads in toilets... ominous fortune cookies. All of that happened before Rhett got his hands on the genie. Why would it have sent messages *before* it was captured?"

Smith stared at Susie.

"What?" she asked.

Brooks stared at Susie.

"It didn't want to be captured by *you* either," Smith said. "This thing has been crying for help for months."

Susie tapped her recorder. "The men have accused me of being a malevolent master to my genie. They say it attempted to summon them to gain its freedom. I find that hard to believe."

"Oh, good. She's narrating again," Brooks said.

Smith looked up at nothing. "Hey, genie. If you're around and we're on the right track, make something wacky happen."

A red balloon appeared, its ribbon in Brooks's hand. He glowered at it and released the ribbon.

Smith watched the balloon float to the ceiling. "I wouldn't call that wacky, but I'll take it—"

KRAKOW. A bolt of lightning struck just outside the window.

Brooks and Smith exchanged worried glances.

"Did you do that?" Brooks asked.

"No. You?"

Brooks shook his head.

"I didn't do it," Susie said.

"We didn't ask," Brooks said.

Smith peered straight ahead, at nothing, and froze in place. "Is anyone else seeing Rhett right now?"

They did. Projected in every mind on the planet was

Rhett's annoying face, with its annoyingly perfect jawline, hairline, and browline.

"Hey, everyone. I have an important announcement," Rhett said. "I'm a djinn—what some would call a genie—and I've been trying to fix the world. I saved the bees. I lowered methane emissions. I got rid of the monsters. One percenters who never gave back? They're dead. I invested in hundreds of companies that are doing great work. They created Imagin, and so much more."

"He has a point," Brooks said. "I still want him dead, though."

Rhett continued. "Some people don't like that I have my hands in so much. Some people don't think it's fair. They're wrong. I just want you all to know... I'm about to make the world a perfect place. And if it's ever not a perfect place, it's the fault of these two. Arturo Brooks and Edward Smith. They're the enemies of progress."

Images of Brooks and Smith appeared in the detectives' own minds, as well as every other mind on Earth.

Smith rolled his eyes. "No one's gonna believe him. You'd have to be an idiot—"

"That was pretty convincing," Susie said.

"You see?" Rhett said. "A magnitude 8.5 earthquake just struck Nepal. *I'd* never let that happen to you, but Arturo Brooks and Edward Smith would. And they did."

Smith sighed. "He's trying to get someone to murder us since he can't."

"We can't hurt him either," Brooks said. "What are we supposed to do?"

"Launch our own propaganda campaign?" Smith suggested.

Susie had another dumb idea. "I can seduce him while you—"

"*No*," Brooks and Smith said.

Smith looked up at nothing again. "Hey, Genie. One

balloon for yes. Two balloons for no. Is there any way we can stop Rhett?"

One balloon appeared in Brooks's hand. He let it float to the ceiling.

"That's promising," Smith said. "Genie. Is there any way to bring Lemon back?"

Again, one balloon appeared in Brooks's hand. He bopped it aside, not feeling particularly uplifted by the news.

Smith pondered. "Genie, can we take Rhett's powers away?"

One balloon. Brooks brushed it away.

"If we do that, will it reverse what he did?"

One balloon. It met the same fate as the others.

"Genie," Smith said. "If we succeed, will I be dead again?"

One balloon. Brooks's heart sank and he released it.

Smith tapped awkwardly at the side of his face, imagining it blown to pieces again. "Well, that's worth it if we get rid of—"

Brooks couldn't take any more. "This is stupid. I'm leaving."

Smith reached for his shoulder. "Where are you going? The genie says we can save Lemon and defeat Rhett—"

Brooks shook himself free. *"For a walk."*

# 36 / DJINN AND TONIC

There were no more good dive bars. Brooklyn real estate being what it was, Smith's best option was Gruff's, a brand new pub designed to look like a dive. The barstools were aluminum trashcans, with cushions made of nothing. Tacky polaroids of the owner with his arm around D-list celebrities—including the entire cast of *Real Gutter Skanks of the Jersey Shore*—lined the walls. High-end, LED Christmas lights illuminated a tap list of overpriced swill.

Smith, sporting red hair and an instant beard to avoid being noticed, eyed the list with indifference. He didn't flirt with the blonde who took a trashcan next to him.

"Water, huh?" Burroughs asked.

"For now." Smith took a sip. "Turo send you?"

Burroughs shook her head. "No. I have no idea where your husband is. Patience told me what happened and there are only a few places you'd be right now."

Smith hung his head in acknowledgment. "Well, you found me. What do you want?"

"I'm sorry, Eddie," said Burroughs.

He shrugged. "It's fine. We can defeat Rhett and get Lemon back. It'll be fine." It sounded almost convincing.

Burroughs leaned in to the bar to get a look at his face. "Then why are you here? Rhett put a hit on you, and you're out in public. Disguised, but still..."

"I'm gonna die again," Smith said. "Don't know if Patience mentioned that. Don't know if Darkstick even told her."

Burroughs's voice showed she wasn't buying it. "You've died before. Why are you here?"

Smith finally looked over, but didn't answer directly. "Every once in a while, Brooksy'll ask me if I've been drinking. You know, whenever I'm miserable or tired or sick or whatever. So far the answer has been no, but I hate that... *that's* where his mind goes. Not to 'are you sick?' or 'what happened?' No. It's always 'have you been drinking?'"

Burroughs didn't understand where his story was going. "So—?"

"What's worse is... I know some day the answer's gonna be yes," Smith said.

"You don't know that."

"I do. It's just a matter of time until I fuck this body up like I did the last one." Smith pointed at himself. "And this? This is the best we can do?"

"What do you mean? You said everything's been great. I heard those words come from your mouth. You can't take them back."

"I mean we've got magic fucking powers and this is the best we can do. I'm an alcoholic, he's an anxious wreck. Lemon's dead. She'll get better. I'm gonna die and get better. This is a woo-woo dreamland and it's still all fucked up."

Burroughs tilted her head. "It is a bit. But why come to a bar if you think the temptation's going to get you?"

"It'll get me either way," Smith said. "Coming here makes it easy to find out if tonight's the night."

As she absorbed that, the bartender took her order: a Manhattan.

If Brooks had been there, he would have given her a "Really?" But Smith shrugged. If Burroughs hadn't ordered something, he would have either given her hell or stormed off for being shown consideration.

"Is tonight the night?" Burroughs asked.

Smith watched the bartender preparing her drink. "Not sure yet."

In his mind, Smith watched Lemon slip into the cracks of the Conner Building over and over. He had every bit of confidence they would fix it, but the image wouldn't shake.

Burroughs saw his eyes sink into despair, and tried to shake him out of it. "So Arturo just... walked out?"

"Yeah. He'll come back. He always comes back. It's just..."

"What?" Burroughs took her drink and nodded at the bartender.

"The part about me dying."

"You've died before." Burroughs shrugged.

"Don't get me wrong. I don't care," Smith said. "It really seemed to set *him* off, though."

"Because you can't cheat death every time. Not forever," Burroughs said.

"Maybe not. But what am I, a catch?" Smith scoffed. "He could have an all-you-can-eat dick buffet with me out of the picture."

Burroughs scrunched her face. "I don't think that's—"

"Or. He's fucking gorgeous. Someone else would marry him." Smith shook his head. "The man's a smart, sexy cyborg. He'll be fine."

"I think you're looking at this wrong," Burroughs said.

"Probably," Smith said.

"Your crazy isn't the same as his crazy," she said. "And I'm not trying to be an asshole because everyone's crazy."

"You sure as shit are." Smith gave a slight, mischievous grin. "What do you mean, though?"

"You—" Burroughs stretched the word looking for the nicest way to say what she meant. "—you expect abuse."

"Should I not? That's what happens."

"I'm not saying you're wrong. I mean, I think you're wrong, but I'm not saying that. I'm saying he knew something different, and his whole life has been a struggle to get back to that high point. Back to the loving family. When he came to me because his memories were messed up, he didn't even care that someone hacked his brain. He was worried he might be crazy. It's all about being normal."

"Yeah, no shit," Smith said.

"Not 'no shit.' I'm saying it's an obsession bordering on

psychosis. I don't know what kind of normal he wants exactly, but I know it's not normal to be a cyborg married to a clone. It's not normal for members of your family to keep dying and coming back to life. It's not normal to get genie powers and rejigger the universe. He wants it to be normal to the point that... he'll do *anything* to make it normal. No offense, Eddie, but that includes getting married when the two of you were *totally* not ready."

"What if things *can't* be normal?" Smith asked. "What if this is it? Scary monsters and super creeps forever."

"Then he might actually go crazy."

Brooks had gone for a walk, and it hadn't calmed him down at all. At the all-new, all-improved Conner Building in midtown Manhattan, he flung open the doors to Rhett's new penthouse. He could have genied into the room, but bursting in felt right. He snapped his fingers and sent Rhett's harem of women to the street below.

"I've had it all wrong," Brooks announced.

"What?" Rhett set down yet another glass of champagne and closed his robe.

Brooks ranted. "All this time, I've been trying to pretend I'm not a cyborg. Hold down a job, have a family, get a dog, go for walks... just live a normal life."

"Go away," Rhett said. "Do I need to kill more of your family?"

"Go ahead," Brooks sneered.

"Excuse me?"

Brooks laughed. "It's going to happen anyway, so you know what? Go ahead."

Rhett scowled. "Could you have your mental breakdown somewhere else? I was having a good time and ending famine over here."

"Kill my family," Brooks said. "Because you know what? I'm a cyborg, and if I don't like it I can erase whatever memories I want. I have reformatting instructions *for my brain*."

"You could wish yourself normal, you know," Rhett said, making a decent point.

"I tried that, and this asshole genie *won't let me*," Brooks said. "But that's fine. It's *fine*. I don't want to be normal anymore. It hasn't happened in ten years and it's never going to happen. So I want to see in the dark. I want to be able to translate books in my head. I want the strength and reflexes to kill you. And I want to make myself forget I ever did it."

Rhett smirked. "I told you, already... you can't kill me."

"You said I can't *use my genie powers* to kill you," Brooks said. "I'm not going to."

Brooks pulled a handgun from his side. Rhett shifted a little, unsure of whether Brooks's technicality was valid. Just in case, he wished Brooks's gun away. In turn, Brooks wished it back. It smoked a little from being pulled in and out of existence.

With his cyborg reflexes, Brooks was able to fire before Rhett could even think to retaliate. Sudden, gushing blood proved Brooks's hunch correct. He fired again. And again. And again. When Rhett lay motionless with a chest full of holes, Brooks stepped closer and fired two more times.

Performing the role of a cool killing machine didn't make him feel like one. Brooks gagged a little and covered his mouth.

*I don't want to see this*, he thought, wishing the gore away.

Nothing happened.

His hands shook a little as he repeated the wish out loud. "Make it go away."

Corpses, though dead, are still abuzz with activity. Bacteria and the laws of physics work in concert to give their insides motion. Accordingly, a gurgling sound came from deep within Rhett's throat.

Brooks's eyes welled up. "I don't want to hear it. I don't want to see it."

Nothing. That was fine. He didn't need genie powers. He'd just do what he promised he would a few moments earlier. He got into his own head to delete the memory of murdering Rhett.

In his HUD, an error popped up:

**You do not have file permissions to do that.**

"Oh God," Brooks said.

His eyes went from the blood on the floor to his trembling hands and back. It was time for him to go a little crazy.

# 37 / DARKNESS

Something was different, and Smith knew it the instant his disguise beard disappeared into thin air. He turned to Burroughs at the bar. In the time it took him to blink, her hair was brown again. He tapped at the crotch of his pants. The magic was gone there as well.

"Spaghetti doesn't have bugs in it, does it?" he asked.

"Um, no?" Burroughs squinted. "Are you sure you've only had water?"

"Shit," Smith said.

He fumbled for his phone and texted Patience:

is maria ok?

As he awaited one of her characteristic, paragraphs-long replies, an incoming call appeared. Brooks. Smith was already worried, but when he picked up and Brooks could barely utter two words, he worried even harder.

"I... got..." Brooks said.

Smith didn't joke. He could hear the fear in his partner's voice. "Where are you?"

Brooks made a whimpering sound and got out a third word. "...the."

"Okay, you're gonna have to give me more than 'the.'"

"I... Rhett..."

Smith raised his voice. "Yeah, I kind of gathered you did something to the genie."

"Just... come here."

Smith still wasn't clear where 'here' was. "Home?"

Brooks mumbled.

"Not home?" Smith asked, like he was trying to get Lassie to show him to a well.

Brooks responded with a few words. Only one was intelligible. "Conner..."

"The Conner Building?" Smith asked.

Brooks mumbled something that seemed affirmative.

"I'm on my way," Smith said. He snapped his finger to leave, but his body remained at Gruff's. "Shit." He hopped off the trashcan and grabbed his coat.

"What's wrong?" Burroughs asked.

Smith was already halfway to the door, and he called back. "I have to go to the Conner Building. Get the tab and meet me there?"

On his way out the door, he snapped his fingers again. Nothing happened. Not having genie powers was a problem. It meant Brooks probably didn't either, and it meant anything that could normally hurt a cyborg could hurt him once again. Smith jogged to the nearest subway station and hoped the forty-minute ride wouldn't feel too long. As he boarded, he received Patience's reply:

I'm afraid I don't know the person to whom you refer.

The Conner Building stood abandoned, not that it ever had anyone in it in the first place. The force field was gone. It seemed like Rhett had been beaten, but if that were the case, surely the entire Conner Building would have disappeared? With the panic and horror in Brooks's voice, Smith wasn't sure what to expect. He bounded into the penthouse, ready to console, congratulate, or fight something. He got to do none of those.

Brooks lay on the floor on his back, in the still-expanding pool of Rhett's blood. His eyes were closed, and for a moment it looked like he too had been shot. Smith rushed to him, expecting the worst. He knelt down. When he couldn't find any wounds, he gave Brooks a little shake. "Babe. You okay?"

With Rhett dead, his magic no longer applied. His body puffed up a little, and not from expanding gases. His hair thinned. His face returned to below average attractiveness. Smith gaped at the transformation as it unfolded.

Brooks's eyes flew open. His mouth opened slightly, ready to say something, but no words came out. He shook his head and closed his eyes again. With them shut, he could almost pretend he wasn't lying where he was.

Smith watched as Rhett's hairline receded into nothing. "You fixed it. No one has genie powers."

Brooks didn't open his eyes to speak. "It didn't fix anything."

"Sure it did," Smith said. "All of his imaginary bimbos are gone. His magic's coming undone. Spaghetti's delicious again."

"Ours is coming undone too," Brooks noted.

"I know," Smith said. "My past is getting more traumatic by the second."

Brooks wasn't the slightest bit amused. "Lemon's still dead. Maria's gone. And now I'm a murderer."

"Yeah. You are," Smith said. In spite of his casual tone, it worried him. They'd killed all sorts of monsters, but never a human being and never for revenge. Rhett—bottle of djinn notwithstanding—had been human.

"Part of me is traumatized right now," Brooks said.

"What's the other part?" Smith wondered.

"It wants me to get back up and gut his corpse."

"Okay. That's a little extreme," Smith said.

"I told you I couldn't take another thing." Brooks opened his eyes and stared into his husband's. "You didn't believe me."

Smith blinked. "What?"

"You didn't believe me. I wanted us to just deal with this

world and you kept pushing." His voice changed to mimic Smith's. "*Oh, we'll solve a mystery. We have to stop the bad guy.* Now everyone's dead and we can't fix it." He snapped his fingers. "Look. Still dead." He snapped them again. Wet blood flicked from his fingers onto his face. "Can't even clean up this damn crime scene." SNAP. SNAP. SNAP. "Everything's broken and it's your fault. I could have brought my family back, and lived in Rhett's reality with world peace and honeybees, but nooooo. *That* wouldn't have been okay."

"Sorry? We've never dealt with a genie before and I'm trying my best here."

"Your best is bullshit. Your ideas are bullshit."

Smith put up his hands. "I don't disagree."

Brooks moved to stand up. "Fight back."

"No. You're pissed and you have every right to be."

Brooks stepped toward Smith and poked his chest with a finger. "*Fight back.*"

"No," Smith said. "I'm not arguing with you while you look like an extra from *The Shining.*"

Brooks snapped, this time figuratively. "Fight back! For God's sake, stand up for yourself. For once in your life, stand up for *something.*"

"I wouldn't be here if I didn't care about something," Smith said. He reached for Brooks's shoulder. "Brooksy—"

"Don't 'Brooksy' me. Our daughters are *dead.*"

"I know. I'm trying to—" Smith's eyes watered and he extended his arm again.

Annoyed, Brooks moved to slap his husband's arm away. But Smith was moving toward him faster than he'd thought. Brooks hit the side of Smith's face. Not at cyborg strength, but enough to sting. A harmless accident, if circumstances were different.

Smith dropped to his knees as his mind took him to a memory that was worse than he'd remembered—right back to being shot in the face. A slap to the side of the face wasn't as bad, obviously, but he couldn't stop himself from clutching the side of his face and gasping for air. That memory triggered other memories. While one part of his mind flashed to horrible sights and sounds, another part knew where he was. It knew what was happening, and forced him to prod around the inside of his mouth with his tongue. He wasn't bleeding. No teeth were missing. His cheeks were still intact. He told himself those facts and talked himself out of panic. "I'm fine. I'm fine."

"I'm *so* sorry," Brooks said. He withdrew his hand to his mouth, ashamed.

Smith picked himself up and faced his husband. "Reality hits like a brick to the fucking face."

"I'm sorry," Brooks repeated.

Smith didn't respond to the apology. He was too busy being overwhelmed with memories, so he instead asked a question. "Remember when the woo-woo doctor told us to think about anything we didn't want to share?"

"Yeah..." Brooks squinted, trying to think of where this line of questioning would go.

"You think of anything?" Smith asked.

"No. I didn't have anything to hide."

"I did," Smith said.

Brooks cringed. Whatever Smith felt the need to hide could only be worse than the litany of abuse. He wasn't sure he wanted to know, but he pressed on anyway. "What was it?"

"The conversion therapy," Smith said.

"I know about that," Brooks said.

"Not that it happened. You know *everything* that's happened." Smith shut his eyes. "The fact that it worked."

Brooks glanced down at himself. "How do you figure?"

"No shit I'm still into dudes. It doesn't *work* work. I mean..."

Brooks tilted his head in confusion.

"I mean... It's been, what? Twenty-five years? It still fucks with my head. Sometimes, I wake up next to you and... I get this feeling I've done something wrong, and... I know I haven't. I know that. But I can't help but think I have. And then I hate myself for not letting it go." Smith sighed. "It's a mess."

"That explains *a lot.* But why are you telling me now?"

"Because it just hit me and I am *not loving* this stroll down fucking Memory Lane. And also because I need you to understand what I'm about to say."

Brooks was puzzled.

Smith gestured at Rhett's sopping corpse. "This is worse. Worse than getting shot in the face. Worse than anything in my past. Worse than the only thing I hid from you."

"How is this worse?" Brooks asked. "He was an asshole who *murdered Lemon.*"

"Because it's *you.* There's always been some excuse. It's evil Puritan programming, or Godwin Zane blackmailing you, or two sets of memories, or a genie fucking with your head, or..."

Brooks sneered. "I don't know if you've noticed, but those are all things that *actually happened to me.*"

"I don't know if *you've* noticed, but I've been tortured. Abused. Shot. Brainwashed." Smith's eye twitched. "Raped, apparently. I watched you die. I watched Lemon die."

"So we're having an excuse-off?" Brooks asked. "Is that what we're doing?"

Smith exhaled sharply. "There's no excuse! You just doubled down on murdering someone and hit me in the face."

"That was an accident—"

"I know. It doesn't matter. I'm making a *point.* I'm a goddamn *wreck* of a human being, but at least I know that. You don't seem to have a clue that your dark side is... really fucking dark."

"I *do* have four sets of memories right now," Brooks said.

Smith pulled at the sides of his hair. "*Stop making excuses. I have been in your head.* Patience's crazy made her get married at eighteen. Darkstick's crazy makes her narrate things. My crazy made me drink and kill myself. Your crazy is a *cold-blooded killer.* Your crazy wants to beat the shit out of me right now. I can see it in your eyes."

"It does." Brooks clenched his fists. "It really does."

"I *know*," Smith said. "But *you* don't want to. So go ahead and bottle up your inner John Wayne Gacy, okay?"

Brooks lowered his head and sighed. "What do you want to do?"

"I wanna clean up this crime scene and then... I don't know. I just know we're not genies anymore and every instinct in me says I'm not letting you go to jail."

"Even after—"

"Even after you hit me, yeah," Smith said. "Stuff your clothes into a trash bag and go clean up in the shower." He snapped his fingers, wishing his powers would come back. They didn't. "Burroughs is on her way here. I'll tell her to bring supplies."

"Fuck," Smith said to himself when Brooks was out of earshot. He rifled around under the kitchen sink, hunting for chemicals. He didn't know if the Conner Building would exist much longer. He didn't know if he would exist much longer, alive and without holes in his face and torso. But keeping busy would keep him from thinking about past and potential horrors, in theory. While Brooks showered, staring straight ahead at nothing, Smith dragged Rhett's body onto a homemade tarp of garbage bags and got to work scrubbing the floor.

At some point, Brooks emerged in a towel and took a seat. He wanted to say something meaningful, something reassuring. But all that emerged was a pathetic "thank you."

Smith scrubbed.

Brooks stared.

Smith scrubbed some more.

An hour into the most uncomfortable of uncomfortable scenarios, there was a knock at the door. TAP-taTAP. Burroughs let herself in and tossed Brooks a duffel bag of replacement clothes. She didn't ask questions.

"That was quick," Smith said.

"Don't get too excited," Burroughs said, looking over her shoulder.

A more slender and annoying figure pushed Burroughs aside and took her place in the doorway.

"I walk into the penthouse. The overwhelming stench of ammonia burns my nose." Susie tapped the stop button on her tape recorder and shrieked, "What have you done!?"

# 38 / GENIE THERAPY

While Brooks pulled on a blood-free pair of pants, Susie rushed over to Rhett's corpse and wailed.

"Dev!" she shouted. "Dev! Dev!"

Smith tossed a roll of paper towels aside and pushed himself up off the floor. "Uh... that's Rhett. Turns out he was ugly before—"

"He wasn't ugly!" Susie shouted. She knelt down and inspected the body. "He was my husband!"

Brooks, still reeling from committing murder as well as the fact that Burroughs had brought him a Hawaiian shirt, was in no mood. "*What?*"

"It was you two all along," Susie said, pointing at Smith, then Brooks. Conspiracy theories involving Dev and the detectives turned over in her mind. Maybe he witnessed a crime and they changed his identity. Maybe he was secretly a member of their organization all along. She spoke her revelation into her tape recorder. "All this time, I thought a monster killed Dev, when it was my rival detectives. I should have known."

"Oh, wow," Brooks said to Smith.

"Are you thinking what I'm thinking?" Smith asked.

"Maybe..." Brooks hesitated. "What are you thinking?"

"That this guy... Dev... faked his death, changed his name, and went out of his way to find a genie so he could get a new face and never see his wife again?"

Brooks blinked. "Yes..."

"It fits with how he treated Solange," Burroughs said.

"*The worst*," Brooks said.

Smith shook his head. "Still shouldn't have killed him, babe."

"Who's Solange?" Susie wondered.

Smith inhaled and raised a hand. "Not it."

Brooks shook his head. "Nope."

Burroughs was it. "Uh. I hate to break it to you, but Rhett... uh, Dev... got remarried."

"He'd never do that," Susie said. She growled and narrated. "The detectives make horrible accusations against Dev. I don't believe them." Her voice broke a little on the last word. She stopped narrating and resumed sobbing. "He made sure me and the kids were taken care of with his life insurance."

Burroughs put an arm around Susie's shoulder and scooped her up. "Honey. No. He was an asshole and a coward."

Susie continued sobbing and intermittently speaking into her tape recorder. As Burroughs escorted her to the couch, the two tracked some of Rhett's blood across the floor. Smith glowered and reached for the roll of paper towels.

SNAP. The trail of blood disappeared, along with Rhett's body.

"That's better," a chipper voice said.

The group looked to the center of the room to see a cheery Vinegret Tolfin, Mind Therapist, in a floor-length floral skirt.

Brooks crossed his arms and muttered to himself. "*Qué ahora?*"

"It took you awhile, but that's all right," Vinegret said. She stretched her arms behind her back.

"The fuck are you talking about?" Smith asked. "When did *you* become a genie?"

Vinegret pretended to count on her fingers. "One... two... three thousand four hundred and eighty-three years ago. It's nice to be corporeal again."

Brooks tensed and stepped menacingly toward her.

"Settle down, dear," Vinegret said. "I think you've had enough violence for one day."

SNAP. Brooks was back in his chair.

Smith sneered, "Lady, you've got about thirty seconds—"

"Until what?" Vinegret asked. "Until you spin your tires for a few months more?"

"What?" Smith asked.

She stared into his eyes. "Do me a favor, would you? Next time you get an ominous set of fortune cookies, give me a call."

"That was you?" Smith asked.

Vinegret explained. "I sent you two a series of messages trying to lure you in before Rhett could capture me, but you never seemed to get it."

"Before..." Smith was confused, and he trailed off.

"Rhett Conner made an appointment for the Success Blaster 5000. It was only a matter of time before he figured me out," Vinegret said.

"You could have just *come to us and asked*," Brooks said.

"I couldn't," Vinegret said. "I cannot find. I have to be found. It's rather a pain sometimes."

Brooks and Smith glared at her.

"*Rather a pain?*" Brooks hissed.

Susie interrupted. "What happened to *my* genie?"

"Oh, dear. You never had one," Vinegret said.

Brooks and Smith exchanged cynical glances.

Susie spoke through sobs. "I didn't?"

Vinegret shook her head. "I created a fake one for you so you wouldn't come looking for me. I needed someone competent on the case."

The sobbing morphed into wailing. Vinegret snapped her fingers and Susie was teleported back home, where her unsupervised children awaited.

Continuing her previous thought, Vinegret turned to Burroughs. "Next time I'll summon you."

"I'm not a detective anymore," Burroughs said.

"You sure, dear? I think you'd have gotten the hint at the decapitated head in the toilet," said Vinegret.

Burroughs smiled a little.

"*How* is that a hint?" Smith asked.

Brooks agreed. "That's not a hint. That's barely an insinuation."

"You're *detectives*," Vinegret said. "Figure it out. In any case, the Obamacare discount worked, in the end."

"*That* was you?" Brooks asked.

Vinegret chuckled. "Come, dear. Do you think there would ever be a discount on health insurance?"

Brooks rubbed at his temples. "I had to kill a man because of you."

"You sure did," Vinegret said. "Sorry."

"You couldn't just make Rhett disappear or teleport him to London or something?" Smith asked.

"I couldn't," Vinegret said. "There are so many rules and regulations, honest to goodness. I can't seek help from humans. I can't seek revenge. I can't stop someone from finding me. You have no idea how tough it is to live like that."

Brooks glared at the genie.

"I do appreciate being freed, though," she said. "Would it help if I erased your memory of killing him?"

"It would," Brooks said. Before she could do so, he added, "But no. I think we learned our lesson about messing with reality."

"*Our* lesson?" Smith mouthed.

Vinegret beamed. "Wonderful. Another couples energy sync success!"

Brooks and Smith stared at her.

"What?" Vinegret asked. "My business is very real, and I don't make promises I can't keep."

Brooks and Smith continued staring at her.

"How would you like me to reward you?" Vinegret asked.

Smith knelt by Brooks's chair and whispered, "What do you think?"

"What are the odds it bites us in the ass if we wish for something?" Brooks asked.

"High," Smith said. "But we can do it for Maria, if—"

Brooks exhaled. "And spend our lives knowing we didn't really earn it?"

"Maybe. I think you know what I'd do," Smith said.

"Yeah. And I think I'm going to listen to you for once," Brooks said.

"You sure?"

Brooks's eyes welled up. "Yeah. This whole genie thing has been nothing but awful."

Vinegret waved at them from across the room. "Hello?"

Brooks and Smith stood and faced her.

"Put it back," Brooks said. "Anything anyone did with genie powers. Whether it was us or Rhett or you. Just... make the world the way it was supposed to be. The way it was three months ago."

"And don't ever fuck with us again," Smith added.

"That's what you both want?" Vinegret asked.

They nodded.

Brooks took a deep breath. "Before you do that—"

"I know just what to do," Vinegret said.

She prepared her strongest woo.

# 39 / THE LAST SUPPER

Brooks and Smith appeared in their kitchen, where a breakfast feast awaited them. Lemon, of course, ignored the waffles, eggs, and sausage in favor of gobbling down a packet of Pop-Tarts. Patience was eerily silent, as mealtime was meant for contemplation. Maria was tucked into her high chair, looking aimlessly at the sky. Widget zigzagged around everyone's feet, hoping someone would drop something.

"You think this is a good idea?" Smith asked.

"Probably not," Brooks said. "If you disappear, I'll go get another clone. But her—"

They'd asked for one last taste of the reality they'd created for themselves, and this was it.

Maria started crying, and Brooks moved toward her—

Silence.

A white haze filled the room. Brooks shut his eyes, afraid to see how much it would take from him. When the haze cleared, Brooks, Smith, Lemon, and Patience gathered around the table, glancing back and forth at each other. Widget planted himself where the high chair had been and barked at the empty space.

"I'm not dead," Smith said. His surprise turned to a pissy frown. "So it wasn't a mugger. The genie *shot me in the face* to get our attention?"

"I think I *was* dead at one point," Lemon said. "Was I just dead?"

Brooks patted her arm. "You were."

"She left all our memories of what happened?" Smith asked.

"She did." Brooks eyed the spot where Maria would have been, if she still existed. He leaned down and rubbed Widget's neck.

"I guess you did say you didn't want to forget," Smith said.

Brooks sighed and turned to Patience. "Are you okay?"

"Hmm. I seem to recall fighting monsters and living to tell the tale."

Lemon's eyes bulged. "The Fear Eliminator. She got the Fear Eliminator."

"You got the Chi Alignment," Brooks said. "I wouldn't look too much into—"

"Chi Alignment *Ultra*," Lemon corrected.

"Whatever," Smith said.

Lemon bounced a little. "She's not afraid of stuff now, you two learned to be on the same page, and my chi is totes aligned. It worked."

Brooks and Smith shared a doubtful look.

"Your chi?" Brooks wondered.

"Are you sure you're not just convincing yourself it worked?" Smith asked.

"I was happy in a band, at first. I was happy doing detective stuff, at first. I was happy being Patience's life coach, at first. I just gotta keep doing new stuff."

"That sounds like... running away from your problems? I don't know..." Brooks's thought got away from him. It was something hokey about being comfortable with one's circumstances, but at this point he had neither the energy nor the moral high ground for a platitude.

"And you know how I can keep trying new stuff?" Lemon asked.

Smith squinted. "By *trying new stuff*?"

"Time machine," Lemon said.

"Jesus Christ," Smith said.

"I might meet him!" Lemon said. She noticed Brooks staring at the emptiness. "Don't worry. This'll still be my home base."

Patience softly cleared her throat. "May I come with you?"

"You wanna?" Lemon asked, confused.

"Hmm. I believe so," Patience said. She looked down at her left hand, where a wedding band still rested around her ring finger. Time travel seemed like a great way to escape her husband.

Smith leaned in toward Brooks. "Did... did the Fear Eliminator actually work?"

"Maybe?"

Smith pulled out his cell phone and aimed it at Patience, ready to take a picture. She shrank in her chair, flinching. "Guess not."

Lemon had no idea what he'd been mumbling about. She squinted. "Huh?"

"Nothing," Brooks and Smith said at once.

"If you want to be a time traveler, we support you," Brooks said.

"Just don't spoil anything or make more immortals or anything stupid," Smith added.

"We'd never!" Lemon said.

If it seems like Brooks and Smith's reaction to Lemon's plan was too casual, that's because it was. Having already traveled through time a few times, Brooks and Smith were aware that the timeline couldn't be altered. There was no danger of paradox in Lemon and Patience gallivanting through the ages, just the risk that their machine would break down and they'd be stuck somewhere. They were adults, and Brooks and Smith had to let them go.

Lemon grabbed Patience's hand and pulled her toward the stairs. "Come on. We need to get started on our bucket lists. I'm gonna be inspired to write *so many songs* about this."

The girls bounded up the stairs, and Widget chased after them. Brooks and Smith were left in the kitchen, stunned.

"Hey," Smith said. "You know how we couldn't agree on anything before?"

"Yeah," Brooks said.

"I know something we agree on now."

"What?" Brooks sniffed.

"Fuck genies."

Brooks gave a slight smile. "Fuck genies."

# 40 / STUNNING FEATS OF INCOMPETENCE

In the restored version of reality, *Donna!* was alive and as popular as ever. Their bags packed and their time machine ready to go, Patience and Lemon sat in the living room waiting for Brooks and Smith to get home and see them off. In the meantime, there was *Donna!*. At the bottom of the screen was the text: "No One Believes My Paranormal Story!"

"Welcome back," Donna! said. "I'm here with Solange Conner."

Solange raised a hand to acknowledge herself.

"We've already heard how Solange's husband did her wrong using a genie, but I'm sure some viewers are having trouble wrapping their minds around that. So my next guest is a paranormal expert who can tell us more. Please welcome a friend of the show... Susie Darkstick!"

The fake studio audience applauded, but Susie didn't take the stage with cheer. She lumbered over to the couch where Solange sat and loomed over her. She turned to scowl at the audience, then resumed scowling at Solange.

"The genie isn't the story," she growled.

"Whoa. It looks like Susie has a twist for us," Donna! said. She already knew that, but she didn't become the number one daytime talk show by not hamming it up.

"The story is Solange turning my perfectly good husband evil," Susie said.

A chorus of gasps overwhelmed the audio as the studio audience lost their computer-generated minds. Shots of people putting their hands over their mouths and raising their arms in disbelief drove the point home.

Susie growled, "I want to know how you did it."

"I didn't do anything," Solange said. "He killed me at one point. Dude was a real misogynist."

"You're lying."

The gasps, growls, and fighting continued. Lemon hit mute.

"I'm glad our lives aren't that messed up," she said.

Patience nodded.

# 41 / RESOLUTION

Since they'd rung in the New Year in a world that didn't exist, Brooks and Smith decided to ring in their return to reality. The nearest holiday was Chinese New Year. Unsure which cultural elements he was allowed to appropriate, Brooks came equipped with standard-issue party horns and confetti poppers. He didn't understand a word spoken in the crowd around him, so he gave a countdown.

"3... 2... 1... Happy Chinese New Year!" He simultaneously blew the horn and shot confetti all over Bayard Street. A few people looked at him with disdain, then resumed celebrating.

2017 was the year of the rooster, and Smith's cock jokes had been unrelenting for days. But he stared at Brooks, tried to make a connection between blowing the horn and the year of the cock, and lost his train of thought. Dismayed, he turned to his partner. "I'm out of jokes."

Brooks rolled his eyes. "*Qué alivio.*"

"It'll come to me," Smith said.

"I don't doubt it..." Brooks got distracted by a mobile billboard as it passed.

DARKNESS STICKING IT TO YOU?
CALL SUSIE DARKSTICK
AND STICK IT BACK
877-GETSTICK
NO PROBLEM TOO SMALL

Brooks took the opportunity to complain. "I don't know what's worse: that Susie Darkstick is still successful or that Donald Trump is still President."

"Probably still the murder," Smith said.

Whatever the worst thing was, it wasn't the fact that they'd lost Maria. Research showed that the infant had never existed, and though Brooks and Smith clearly remembered her and mourned her loss, it was hard to remain worked up about something that was #FakeReality.*

A dragon dance weaved through the crowd, and the two men moved out of the way. As they leaned against a wall, a small child in an elaborate silk costume approached with a basket of bubble-blowers.

Smith accepted the gift and blew a bubble. He turned to Brooks. "So, what's your new New Year's resolution?"

"To not murder anyone?" Brooks said dryly.

Smith cringed a little and tossed the bubbles. "It's not funny after you've actually done it."

"See? I told you."

"Really, though. What's your resolution?"

"I... am going to work on embracing my real life. I'm a cyborg, and the world is screwy, and that has to be okay." It didn't feel okay, but that's why it was a resolution. "You?"

"Fuck that. I don't make resolutions," Smith said.

Brooks threw up a hand. "After you made me make one?"

"I didn't make you do anything. You would have anyway."

"Yeah, but still."

"Fine. Uh..." Smith's eyes narrowed. "I resolve to believe you."

"What?"

Smith pointed at himself with both hands. "Historically? Not a good listener." He lowered his hands. "When you tell me you want to get married, or that I'm incredibly fucked and need therapy, or that the entire world has been borked by a genie, or that you're about to snap and murder someone, or whatever... I'll believe you."

"Whatever I say?" Brooks raised his brow.

---

* They were actually devastated, but sixty pages of gross sobbing and couple's therapy don't belong in a comedy.

"Yes?" Smith tilted his head suspiciously. "You're not gonna tell me the tap water made you gay, are you?"

Brooks laughed. "No."

"Then I'll believe whatever you say."

"Then I'll say... I love you, and—"

Smith groaned at the verbal PDA. "You're the worst—"

"—*and* that's worth dealing with everything we deal with."

Smith's eyes widened with epiphany. "That's it."

"What's what?" Brooks asked.

"The hackneyed slogan," Smith said. "You just said it."

"I did?"

Smith rolled his hand in the air as he rearranged the words in his mind. "The things you love are worth it. Some bullshit like that."

Brooks's eyes widened. "We're a premium brand."

"Right. We can't compete with free, so we *guilt* people into paying." Smith put on a soft, announcer-style voice. "You wouldn't trust a bargain doctor with your loved ones' lives, so why trust a bargain detective agency?"

"Yes!" Brooks lowered his head in shame. "I feel dirty."

"Not as dirty as you're gonna feel in a few hours." Smith winked.

Brooks sighed to himself. "*Eres el peor.*"

"Nah, I'm not the worst," Smith said.

Brooks's face went blank. "I... I know. I was acting exasperated."

"No, I know," Smith said. "It's just... I usually agree with you." He was taken aback by his own words. "I don't right now."

Brooks's eyes widened. "Do... do you like yourself now?"

Smith snorted. "No. But if we keep meeting assholes, I might. I mean... I think I look pretty damn good next to Rhett and Vinegret and Darkstick."

"You've always looked pretty damn good," Brooks said.

Smith groaned again.

Brooks held up a finger to interrupt him before he could say anything. "You said you'd believe me! Anything I said."

"And *you* said you'd embrace being a cyborg."

"Yeah? So?"

Smith moved in close. "So read my vitals and tell me the fastest way home."

Brooks smiled at the first question and obliged the second. "The C."

"The C it is, then."

Smith roped an arm around Brooks and they headed toward the station.

One cute conversation and a few resolutions didn't make their lives perfect. Nothing could. But Brooks and Smith finally had a place to start. Everything was broken until the genie came along and ruined everything.

## ACKNOWLEDGEMENTS

I'd like to thank all the usual suspects (Ellen, Adam, Lianna-bob, family, friends, framily...). I'd also like to thank my dozen fans. As a millennial whose entire sense of self-worth is based on praise, hearing from you makes my day more than eating avocado toast and failing to save for retirement ever could. If you want to bring me even more joy, leave a review on Amazon or Goodreads. Just a thought. Take it or leave it.

Brooks and Smith return in:
*Fun Times in a Dystopic Hellscape (Book 4)*

Susie Darkstick will never return.

For announcements about new projects,
sign up for the mailing list at martina-fetzer.com, or
scan this little QR code...